THE YEAR OF THE DRAGON

L.A. private investigator Mike Faraday
is hired by a millionaire midget to
trace Dale, his six-foot-tall daughter.
But is Jack Larsen telling the truth?
Is Dale, who had decamped with a
fortune, really his daughter? Jack is
not the only one looking for Dale, and
in his investigations, Faraday meets
allsorts, including a poisonous snake
and a panther.

Books by Basil Copper
in the Linford Mystery Library:

THE HIGH WALL
HARD CONTRACT
STRONG-ARM
SNOW-JOB
A GOOD PLACE TO DIE
THE NARROW CORNER
JET-LAG
TUXEDO PARK
DEAD FILE
BAD SCENE

BASIL COPPER

THE
YEAR OF
THE DRAGON

Complete and Unabridged

LINFORD
Leicester

First published in Great Britain in 1977 by
Robert Hale Limited
London

First Linford Edition
published August 1991

British Library CIP Data

Copper, Basil *1924* –
    The year of the dragon. — Large print ed. —
    Linford mystery library
    I. Title
    823.914 [F]

    ISBN 0–7089–7077–X

Published by
F. A. Thorpe (Publishing) Ltd.
Anstey, Leicestershire

Set by Words & Graphics Ltd.
Anstey, Leicestershire
Printed and bound in Great Britain by
T. J. Press (Padstow) Ltd., Padstow, Cornwall

This one is for
Winifred Edwards
an ever gracious
lady, whose friendship
I value

1

IT was hot. Not only hot but sticky with it. That's the worst kind of heat. The sort that bounces up from manhole covers and scorches through the soles of one's feet. That sets a clean shirt clinging limply round one's armpits; that makes the sidewalk shimmer and buckle in the frying atmosphere; and where the smog hangs choking in the throat and deposits gritty fragments on the windshield.

Don't get me wrong. L.A.'s a fine town. But it's a fine town to be out of in such weather. I could have done with being up in the hills right now, with an emerald-blue lake at my feet and a stein of iced beer in my right hand. I sighed and put the thought to the back of my mind. You're getting old, Faraday, I told myself. I tell myself that at least once a week these days. It's one of the penalties

1

of being thirty-three.

I tooled my old powder-blue Buick off the main-stem and bumped over the side-road of Ticonderoga Drive. The palm fronds cut up chunks of dazzling blue sky and threw jagged shadows across the road. The dust drifted in and settled on the upholstery like snow. A tall man in a stetson and riding a chestnut loomed up in the centre of the windshield; he looked dry and leathery and part of the landscape. For a minute I thought it was Tom Mix back again.

I grinned and watched him disappear in the rear mirror. That would have dated me. Stella probably hadn't even heard of Tom Mix. Unless she'd been watching some prehistoric footage on TV.

I found the lane I wanted and drew up in front of tall iron gates hung from stone pillars. There was a white stucco lodge with green Spanish tiles at one side and an enormous man in a blue sweat-stained shirt standing in the lodge doorway. I couldn't see the rest of him because he was in deep shadow. He eased out as I

2

stopped the Buick and gave me a hard look with his narrow eyes.

He wore faded blue jeans tucked into top-boots and a heavy black leather belt buckled round his waist. I say waist advisedly. It looked more like a peninsula. He must have weighed about eighteen stones. His angry-looking red face was beaded with sweat that ran down in rivulets from among the roots of his dark curly hair.

He had a pair of black cheaters pushed up on his forehead to examine me better. Now he put them down over his eyes; the addition of the glasses made his face look blank and menacing. He came over to the bars of the gate and glanced at me incuriously.

"You must be the man," he said in a high, soft voice.

"Mike Faraday to see Jack Larsen," I said.

The man-mountain grunted.

"Mr Larsen," he said.

"You call him what you like," I said. "He's not my employer."

3

The big man sucked his teeth in over his lip with an unpleasant noise.

"He will be if you take the job," he said equably. "You got some identification?"

I found one of our best cards; those with the curlicue script and the deckle edges. I got out the car and handed it to him through the bars. He looked at home behind them, come to think of it.

"Faraday Investigations, eh?"

"That's what it says," I told him.

He was already unlocking the gates as I got in the car. I drove in and waited while he closed them behind me. He came back and rested a hand like a leg of pork on the edge of the door.

"Just keep going up the drive," he said. "Someone will meet you at the foot of the steps. Don't get out the car until you're invited. They got lots of nasty things crawling around the grounds."

"Sounds like a nice set-up," I said.

"We like it," the giant said.

He waved me on and stepped back as I gunned the motor. I drove on in a series of long straights with right-angle

4

turns until I came to the house. It was a big spread, high-up with about two acres of lawn in front of it. There were sprinklers going every few yards and the air blowing over and through the spray made the atmosphere a little more bearable. A tall, thin man in an impeccably cut midnight blue suit was waiting for me at the bottom of a flight of marble steps that spiralled upward from the gravel concourse.

He had glossy black hair, a smooth open face, deeply tanned and glossy manners to go with the hair. He held out a hard fist for me to shake as I got out the car.

"Glad you could make it, Mr Faraday. Greg Lauritzen. I'm Mr Larsen's right-hand man. He's expecting you."

He led the way up the steps with an easy, loping grace. I was in a lather of perspiration before I got to the top. There wasn't even a shine on his mirror-smooth brow. He looked at me satirically.

"It is a little hot, Mr Faraday. Perhaps you'd like something long and cool

5

before you go in to see Mr Larsen. I think we have a few minutes."

"That would be fine," I said.

He led the way over past the heart-shaped swim pool, deserted now, its bluey-green water reflecting back the brilliance of the sun. The place was just a little bigger than The White House and only a little less ostentatious. Think of a French chateau crossed with the Taj Mahal and you wouldn't be far off. We sat down in long cane chairs in a shady part of the patio where a cool breeze blew from off the water. I blinked up at the green onion domes in the background and waited for Joe Stalin to kick us off the terrace.

Instead, a Japanese houseboy in deep scarlet livery fussed about with long glasses, limes and cracked ice. I felt some of the heat of the day being washed away as I looked at the cool beading of moisture on the glass. Lauritzen stared at me over the rim of his own glass and made an appreciative smacking noise.

"What's your business with Mr Larsen, Mr Faraday?"

I stared at him.

"Don't you know?" I said.

Lauritzen stared at me in turn. He shook his head.

"He didn't say on this occasion. As I handle most of his affairs I was naturally curious."

I shrugged.

"I was just asked to come out here. So I came."

Lauritzen set his glass down on a crystal tray that stood on the round table between the wicker chairs. The house-boy was out of ear-shot but he hovered in the background in case he was needed.

"I understand you're a private invest-igator, Mr Faraday."

I nodded.

"That's right. People usually send for me when they're in some sort of trouble. The sort of trouble they don't want the official police mixed up in."

Lauritzen gave me a cracked grin. A

7

tiny droplet of moisture was showing near the hair-line. It was the only sign he'd so far given that it was a warm day.

"There are a number of reasons Mr Larsen might want your services, Mr Faraday."

"Maybe we'll find out when I come back from seeing Mr Larsen," I said.

Lauritzen gave me a sharp look from his deep brown eyes.

"Don't get me wrong, Mr Faraday. I just take orders around here. Mr Larsen's a big man in the fields in which he chooses to operate. If he wants to tell me about your visit he'll tell me. I wasn't suggesting anything . . . "

"I haven't said you were, Mr Lauritzen," I told him.

I took another long cool drag at the drink. I was beginning to feel like a human being again. I looked at him curiously.

"But at the same time you can't help being human. So it won't stop you from asking what Mr Larsen wanted when I come out?"

Lauritzen grinned. He struck his thigh with the flat of his hand. It made a resounding crack in the steamy silence of the terrace.

"Like hell it won't, Mr Faraday!" he said. "You catch on quick. We'll do business together all right."

I didn't answer that but sat and finished my drink until it was time to see Larsen. It was just coming up to three o'clock when Lauritzen stood up with a grunt. He gave a quick glance at his watch.

"Mr Larsen's pretty hot on time, Mr Faraday. I'll show you in now, if you're ready."

"Ready as I'll ever be," I said.

We went up the terrace and in through some French windows. We crossed over the parquet floor of a big library which looked musty and neglected. I guessed then maybe the house had been rented. Lauritzen took me along a short corridor and through a pine-panelled den that had elks heads and other horned trophies mounted on the walls. He rapped at a heavy oak door and waited. Then he nodded at me, opened the door and ushered me through.

The high-ceilinged room was a blaze of light. The sun, reflecting from off the terrace outside came clear through big oval windows. The windows were tightly closed but louvres were open at the tops to get the breeze. They were fitted with Venetian blinds but they were rolled up on their cords.

The room was like a replica of something out of the eighteenth century; the elaborate plaster ceiling was picked out in gold and chocolate brown. There was a massive marble fireplace that might been an Adam imported from England and oil paintings in heavy gold frames on the walls. The paintings looked genuine too but the fierce Californian sunlight falling direct on to the canvas wasn't doing them any good.

The walls were pale green and there were big walnut tables set about. A bar had been fitted up at one side which spoiled the proportions of the room and looked completely out of place. That wasn't the only thing that had been altered. The carpet had been removed, leaving a huge golden oblong on the parquet. A hi-fi outfit was blaring away; the volume was so high that when I got to the far end of the room I couldn't hear what language the vocalist was singing in. It wouldn't have mattered anyway.

The man sitting at the bar must have cut a switch as I came up toward him because the noise suddenly dribbled into silence. The bar wasn't the only incongruous thing in the room. There were pin-tables lined up in a double row where the carpet had been. They were all kinds of games and they were all wired up for operation; sheaths of thin grey cable were festooned across the floor and draped over chairs. There were fruit machines too and on a low, long Louis Quatorze table were heaped piles of coins. I expected Jack Larsen to be pretty bizarre but he was the most incongruous thing in the room.

For a start he was only about three feet tall. He wasn't a dwarf because he was perfectly proportioned; to hide or at least camouflage his midget stature he sat on top of a high stool at the bar which made his head come up to the level of the average person. I didn't notice that until I was almost up to him and it was quite a shock.

He was about thirty-five, I should have said and had glossy black hair that was shining with brilliantine. He had a thin, heavily tanned face and deep-set eyes that were half-hidden beneath sandy eye-lashes. The pupils were almost black. The face wasn't bad-looking but was spoiled by the thin lips and the expressionless mouth.

He didn't move from the bar but gave me a limp hand to shake as I came up. His face hadn't changed expression but he was looking me carefully over. There was a half-smoked cigar in a crystal tray at his elbow and a glass of what looked like orange juice in front of him. Later I found out he drunk nothing else; either the bar was for show or for the benefit of guests.

He had scarlet leather carpet slippers on his feet and wore a blue, open-neck shirt under a red and white towelling bath-robe he had belted tightly at the waist. He wasn't the most amazing-looking client I'd ever had but he would do until I could remember one.

"Would you like a drink, Mr Faraday?"

The voice was like a buzz-saw cutting through sandpaper. The brittle, metallic quality of the voice, combined with the tight lips had gotten the man where he was. That and the will in the tiny body. Whether the quality of the life the man had achieved for himself was worthwhile was another matter. I wasn't there to make value judgements.

I shook my head.

"It's a bit early in the day, Mr Larsen. But I could use something long and cool with ice in it."

The little man had an amused expression on his face. He jerked with an expressive thumb over to the back of the bar.

"Help yourself. Everything's refrigerated in back. The minerals are on the bottom shelf."

I went around and did like he said. The wood-grained lockers had ice-boxes behind them. I got a carton of fresh orange-juice and poured it into the long frosted glass. I closed the door and went on back to where Larsen sat. He hadn't moved and he had his eyes half-closed like he was thinking out his dialogue. I pulled over one of the high stools and sat at the bar next him. I tried the orange-juice. It tasted great. He opened his eyes and the black pupils stared into mine.

"I'm glad you said that, Mr Faraday. I like a man who's choosy about his drinking habits. This isn't a job for any juiced-up private dick. I guess I heard right about you."

I didn't bother to answer that but went on sipping my drink and waiting for him to continue. He got tired in the end and started up again.

"You got credentials, Mr Faraday?"

"Sure," I said.

I slid the photostat of my licence in the plastic holder over to him and watched his face as he studied it. His lips moved soundlessly like those of a man just learning to read. He flipped it back and focused his eyes up on my toe-caps.

"You were recommended, Mr Faraday. Very highly recommended."

I stared at him.

"That's nice to know, Mr Larsen. By whom, for instance?"

Larsen drew a bluish tongue across his lips with a quick snake-like movement.

"That's restricted information, Mr Faraday."

"What's the problem?" I said.

Larsen sighed.

"I'm just coming to it."

He reached over for a heavy buff envelope on the bar in front of him. He took out some papers and a batch of glossy photographs. He riffled through

15

them with a thick forefinger.

"My daughter's run away, Mr Faraday. Not to mince matters, we had a quarrel. I want her back."

"Have you tried Missing Persons?" I said.

Larsen had a shocked look on his face. He made an irritated clicking noise with his tongue.

"I don't operate like that, Mr Faraday. This is a confidential matter. Which is why I wanted a high-class operative. Someone who can keep his lip buttoned in return for top dollar."

I shrugged.

"You got a picture?"

Larsen nodded.

"Sure. Right here."

I got out a small notebook and a pencil. Larsen stiffened.

"Nothing in writing, Mr Faraday. Keep it up there."

He tapped his forehead. I put the notebook away and waited for him to go on.

"She went missing three weeks ago,"

he said. "Since then I've heard nothing. It's happened before but I heard within two-three days. She's just turned eighteen. And wild. Very wild indeed."

"Where am I supposed to look?" I said.

Larsen turned his black pupils on me.

"She'll be in L.A. somewhere, Mr Faraday. Dale's a dancer.

"Shouldn't take me more than a year," I said. "Miss Dale Larsen, 18, a dancer . . ."

Larsen interrupted me. He stabbed the air with his forefinger. For some reason the gesture held an air of hidden menace. It reminded me of something.

"Dale Holden," Larsen grated. "That's her professional name. I can give you a short-list of spots she might operate from. Clubs and such-like."

I nodded. I studied the glossy Larsen shoved over to me. The girl was a honey, all right. Honey-blonde to be exact. It was a professional picture, probably cut from the end of a chorus line; the girl was wearing mainly feathers and a bright

17

smile. She must have been a big girl too; nearly six feet, I should have said. I looked at Larsen thoughtfully.

"What's the rest of the story?"

"This kid's wild enough for anything, Mr Faraday," he said. "My biggest worry is her shooting off her mouth. I have business rivals; a lot of people who'd like to put the bite on me. Supposing Dale got snatched while she's running around loose. Three or four million dollars is the going rate for ransom in these cases, isn't it?"

I looked at him for a long moment.

"Sounds a bit far-fetched, Mr Larsen. The girl just took off after a family tiff . . . "

Larsen shook his head.

"Happens all the time, Mr Faraday."

He had a point there.

"Nice to know you've got three million dollars, Mr Larsen," I said.

Larsen gave me a crooked grin.

"I like your cut, Mr Faraday. But you're wrong about the money. I got far more than three million dollars. And it brings plenty troubles, believe me."

"I'm bleeding all over your rug," I said.

Larsen chuckled. His laugh had the same rusty-tin quality as his voice.

"We'll get along fine, Mr Faraday."

He reached out for a cheque-book with mauve leaves. He scribbled something in it with quick, nervous strokes. He threw the cheque across to me.

"There's a thousand dollars for starters. If you want any more for expenses, let me know."

I sighed. It had been a rough season. I put the cheque in my bill-fold. It seemed to burn a hole in the leather.

"I think we can do business, Mr Larsen," I said.

2

I WALKED to the door. Larsen stood by the bar, watching me. "Not a word to anyone about this," he said sharply.

"Not even to Mr Lauritzen?"

Larsen shut his mouth in a ferocious scowl.

"Specially Mr Lauritzen," he gritted.

"Got you," I said.

I went on out, closing the door behind me. I walked down the corridor. Lauritzen was lounging in what was meant to be a casual pose against a leather chair in the pine-panelled room got up as a den. I jerked my thumb toward Larsen's door.

"He wants to see you," I said.

Lauritzen gave me a startled look. He went at a run down the corridor.

"Hang around, Mr Faraday," he said over his shoulder. "I want to talk to you when I get back."

I grinned. I went on out through the French windows, past the heart-shaped swim pool, across the lawns with the sprinklers and back down the marble steps that spiralled to the concourse. I got in the Buick, wincing at the heat of the cushions across my shoulders. I put the cardboard-backed envelope with the print of Dale Holden in the dash cubby and locked it. I lit a cigarette and was just starting the engine when Lauritzen came down the steps. He looked angry and he was in a lather of sweat this time.

"Mr Larsen didn't want me," he said accusingly.

"Must have been my mistake," I said.

I smiled politely and started to put the car in gear.

"You didn't tell me anything," he said.

"You didn't tell me Mr Larsen was a midget," I told him. "The shock might have been fatal with my frail health."

His mouth was still open as I gunned on out. I drove on down to the main gate. The big man in the private army outfit was lounging outside the lodge. He already had the gate open before I got there. I noticed, coming round the last bend there was a large animal on the grass near the shrubbery which bordered the drive. There was a glint of a chain as it moved; I stared disbelievingly. It looked like a panther. It was too big for a dog.

The man with the guts, the red face and the dark glasses put up his hand so I stopped. He looked the Buick over like he thought I might have Jack Larsen in the glove-compartment. I might have at that.

"So you got to see the man, eh?" he said in his high, soft voice.

"Sure," I said. "If it's John Wayne you're talking about."

The big man snickered to himself.

"That's a good one. Well, I guess it's all right for you to leave. Don't do anything I wouldn't."

"That gives me a wide field," I said. "What's the wild life for?"

The big man sniggered again.

"We're putting on a circus in the fall," he said. "We already got the midget."

"And a clown at the front gate," I said. "Should be a sell-out."

I tooled the Buick out through the entrance before he could think of a comeback. The grin on my face lasted me all the way to the office. I stashed the Buick in my usual garage and walked back to our building. I rode up in the creaky elevator. The place had the atmosphere it always has; made up of stale floor polish and poor air-conditioning. Still, it was the nearest we had to home. I heard Stella's typewriter going long before I got to the waiting room door.

The door of the inner office was open and I heard Stella get up and go across to the glassed-in cubicle where we do the brewing up. The typing started again almost as soon as I heard the snick of the percolator. I grinned. I went on in and shut the door behind me.

"You're taking me for granted, honey," I said.

Stella smiled. She wore a patterned silk dress today with a short skirt and her hair shone like a gold bell underneath the lamps. She turned very blue eyes toward me.

"Since when did you not want coffee?"

I didn't bother to answer that. I went over to my old broadtop and sat down in the swivel chair and looked at Stella. She flushed beneath the tan. She must have guessed what I was thinking. My thoughts were pretty transparent where Stella was concerned, anyway. She went back over and fussed around with cups and saucers. I admired her action all the way to the alcove. Then I switched to the cracks in the ceiling. It was too hot for those sort of thoughts today.

"How did you get on with Jack Larsen?" Stella said.

I lit a cigarette and put the spent match-stalk in the tray on my desk.

"He wants me to find his missing daughter," I said.

Stella came over behind me and stood looking down at the brown envelope I'd put on the blotter. I drew out the picture of Dale Holden.

"A nice big girl," she said drily.

"Considering her father's a midget," I said.

Stella came around to the side and stared at me blankly.

"He stands about three feet nothing in his stockinged feet," I said.

"That must have been unnerving," Stella said.

"It was," I told her.

I frowned at the picture while Stella went over to fetch the coffee. She carried her own over to her desk and sat fooling with that morning's copy of the *Examiner*. I sat inhaling the aroma of roast coffee beans and enjoying one of the best moments of the day.

"It's the Year of the Dragon," Stella said, rustling the paper.

"Big deal," I said.

She frowned.

"It's a Chinese horoscope, you goof.

It's supposed to bring good luck."

"It brought something better than that." I said.

I opened up my wallet and got out Larsen's cheque. I made it into a little dart and skimmed it in Stella's direction. She put up an expert hand up and caught it in mid-flight. I saw the shocked disbelief on her face as she smoothed it out.

"What did you do to get this? Beat it out of him?"

I looked reproachfully at Stella.

"Even I draw the line at roughing up midgets," I said. "Besides, he's a financial heavyweight."

"Sorry," Stella said.

She looked at the cheque with a dreamy eye.

"I'd better put this in the account first thing in the morning before he changes his mind."

I grinned. I went on sipping the coffee and looking at the cracks in the ceiling, my mind a blank. It's a blank at the best of times but this was the perfect moment of the day for it. Stella had another sudden burst of energy. She attacked the typewriter ferociously and then slid the paper out the roller. She checked it over and brought the letter over for me to sign. I scribbled my name at the bottom. Stella sighed.

"Aren't you going to read it?"

"What's the point, honey?" I said. "It's never less than perfect."

Stella gave me a strange look with those unnerving blue eyes.

"What are you after? That was a gross piece of flattery, even for you."

She went over to her desk, folded the letter and sealed it in an envelope. Then she went to the wall-safe, the one we keep behind the large-scale map of L.A. and stashed the cheque.

"Don't forget the combination," I said.

Stella looked at me mischievously.

"That'll be the day," she said.

She went back to her desk, hooded the typewriter, stacked the letters and sat down to her coffee again.

"So what's with Dale Holden?"

"She had a quarrel with the old man and walked out," I said. "He wants me to bring her back."

Stella glanced down at the picture of the girl; she'd taken it over to her own desk to enter details in her notebook.

"Any leads?"

"He's given me some addresses of clubs and spots around town where I might get a line," I said. "She's a dancer."

"It figures," Stella said. "She hasn't got the build or the style of a high school teacher."

"I don't know," I said. "I knew a high school teacher once . . ."

"Spare us the details," Stella interrupted. She got up and took my cup. She skipped out before I could grab her and went over to the alcove. I sat back and lit a cigarette and listened to the faint hum of the stalled traffic on the boulevard and watched the blue, green and red stripes the neon was making in the dusk. Stella came back and put the filled cup down on my blotter.

"How are you fixed for food tonight, Mike?"

"Depends on your finances, honey," I said.

Stella made a moue.

"Mean as ever," she told the filing cabinet.

She looked thoughtfully over at the map of L.A. on the far wall.

"I think I can manage now there's a new cash-flow coming into the firm."

"Great," I said. "I'm your man."

Stella went round and stood looking down at the print of Dale Holden.

"What about Jack Larsen's commission?"

I grinned.

"We begin spending his money tonight and make a start on the case in the morning," I said.

3

MULLER'S Theatrical Agency was a frayed at the edges set-up which occupied several large rooms on a cross-town location. I walked up three flights of stairs knee-deep in candy wrappers and peanut shucks and fought my way across a dusty carpet to the reception area. There was nobody in the waiting room nobody, that is, if you excepted a faded colour print of Ramon Novarro hanging on one wall: and a slightly more-up-to-date black and white study of Clark Gable on the other.

Gable was squinting into the sun and looking like he might be studying his pay-check for Gone With the Wind. In both cases the implication was that Novarro and Gable had been former clients of the agency. I thought it extremely unlikely to say the least. There was no-one around. There was a copy of that morning's *Examiner* sitting atop the dusty counter and a cold cup of coffee in a transparent beaker getting colder next to it. The only sign of life was a plastic-bladed fan which was redistributing the dust.

I punched the button of the bell on the counter and waited for its cracked echoes to die away. There was a faint shuffling in the distance but nothing happened so I hit the bell again. This time the floor vibrated. I looked across at Gable and winked sympathetically. I waited for the footsteps to drag their way across to me.

A severe-looking woman with iron grey hair cut like a man eased through the doorway. Her face didn't exactly crack up with pleasure when she saw me. She wore gold-framed eye-glasses and had a dead cigarette butt stuck in the corner of her mouth. She reminded me of Ned Sparks but I didn't tell her that.

"Yes?"

The voice had the harsh, dead quality

31

of wind blowing through rusty tin fencing. It didn't endear her to me.

"I'd like to speak to Mr Muller," I said.

She looked me up and down sourly.

"You'll need a ouija-board," she said. "Muller fell under a street-car, four-five years ago."

"Hard luck," I said.

"It was for him," the grey-haired woman said, shifting gear on the cigarette in the corner of her mouth.

"Perhaps you've got somebody more recent who would do."

The woman finished easing through the door and came across toward me. I blinked. She wore bright mauve trousers and an orange sweater. I looked for the drum-majorette's baton but I guessed she'd left it home today.

"What do you want?"

"Information," I said.

She blinked again warily. The iron-grey eyes matched her hair nicely. I tried to avoid the shrieking dissonance of her costume and concentrated on the dialogue instead. I got out the photostat and showed it her. She just jerked her eyes downward and took in the information. Her expression didn't change.

"I'm Dora Farrow. I run the Agency now. What can I do for you, Mr Faraday?"

"I'm looking for a young girl," I said. Dora Farrow sighed.

"Who isn't?" she said, shifting gear on the cigarette again.

"Don't misunderstand me, Miss Farrow," I said. "This is strictly business."

The grey-haired woman went around the counter and seated herself on a stool. That gave my eyes a little rest. Now only the top half of her looked like a Turner sunset. The corners of her mouth relaxed.

"That's what they all say," she told the peeling wallpaper.

I got out the picture and showed it to her. She let out her breath in a long whistle.

"Some looker. What did you say her name was?"

"I didn't," I said. "But for the record, it's Dale Holden."

The grey woman shook her head.

"I'd remember her all right. She ain't on our books. What's she done? Got herself enticed into a cat-house?"

I shook my head.

"Nothing like that. Just a simple missing persons. There's some folding stuff if you're helpful."

The grey eyes were alive now. They looked at me shrewdly.

"How much folding stuff?"

"Depends how helpful you are," I said.

The eyes looked regretful. She reached under the counter and came up with a big black leather index book. She riffled through it without enthusiasm, muttering to herself.

"I always like to help the law," she said.

"I'm not the law," I said.

Dora Farrow looked at me over her gold-rimmed glasses. She licked her thin lips.

"You look a whole lot better to me," she said.

"I'll top it by ten dollars for the flattery," I said.

Dora Farrow came the nearest to a smile I'd yet seen. She snapped the leather-bound book shut and rummaged around in a cardboard folder she produced from somewhere else under the counter. She was breathing wheezily through the nose now as she concentrated.

She finished fiddling about with pieces of paper and shook her head.

"It's no use, Mr Faraday. I can't come close to her. Not with those looks.

She squinted at the picture again.

"Unless she changed her name. And used a dark wig."

"I didn't expect to strike pay-dirt first off," I said.

Dora Farrow held up her hand with a peremptory gesture.

"I haven't finished yet, Mr Faraday."

She was looking at a grimy piece of paper, shaking her head.

"You know a spot called The Crazy

Horse? Over on the other side of town?"

"I heard of it," I said. "I can find it all right."

Dora Farrow nodded. Her grey eyes stared at me thoughtfully.

"There's a barman there called Dexter. He knows just about everybody in show business in California. He keeps cuttings. It's a sort of hobby."

"I'm obliged," I said.

Dora Farrow took the bills and looked at them sadly.

"I was only leading you on, Mr Faraday. I'm not that hard up."

She stuffed the bills back into the top of my jacket pocket.

"The information was worth it," I said. "It could cut corners. And it comes out of expenses."

The grey-haired woman shook her head slowly.

"Save your money, Mr Faraday. Dexter doesn't come cheap. It will cost you if you do business with him."

"How much?"

Dora Farrow shrugged her shoulders.

"You'll have to make your own arrangements. But I hear he charges a hundred dollars upwards for his tips, according to value."

I took the bills out my pocket and put them back in my wallet.

"That's a bit rich for the sort of case I'm on," I said.

That didn't fool the old lady one bit.

"Don't try to get smart with me, Mr Faraday," she said gently. "Dexter could save you several weeks' foot-work. And he always comes up. No results, no fee."

I grinned.

"Fair enough. Thanks again."

I left her standing behind the counter, the cigarette still clamped in the corner of her mouth. The phone shrilled as I went down the stairs. It sounded like a trumpet-solo in a morgue. I got the Buick and started making tracks toward Dexter.

The Crazy Horse was a big place that had seen better days. Some of the sections were missing from the neon signs; the stucco on the façade was chipped and peeling; and the faded sun-shades that flapped heavily in the scorching currents of air needed replacing.

I drove the Buick in between the tall plaster statues of bucking horses and parked in rear of a maroon Maserati with twin exhausts. I didn't hang around long. It would have only made me envious. The heap probably belonged to one of the cleaners anyway. I grinned to myself as I went up the steps and in through the big glass doors. You're getting cynical, Faraday, I told myself.

Muzak was dribbling from concealed speakers in the lobby, which was cream and gold, and there was a faint, stale sell that all these places have; composed mainly of cheap perfume, sweat and cigarette smoke. There was no-one around but a vacuum cleaner was going in one of the corridors. I went over and glanced in through the main doors that led off the lobby. The big restaurant was empty.

It was dark in here so I waited for my

eyes to adjust and went on over to the far corner where there was a staircase with MEZZANINE BAR in gold letters over it. I got up the stairs and came out on another broad landing. A waiter in a midnight blue jacket passed me on the way down. I called after him.

"I'm looking for a character called Dexter."

He jerked his thumb back over his shoulder without turning.

"In the bar, Mister. He's just come on."

I opened my mouth to thank him but he'd already disappeared. I pushed open the iron rococo door in front of me. The bar was a long one and part of the curved mezzanine which overlooked the gaming tables down below. A tall, dark-haired man of about forty was sitting at a stool behind the bar, rinsing glasses in a stainless steel sink and humming to himself through the cigarette-end jammed in his mouth. He reminded me of the woman at the talent agency.

He didn't look up as I came down the

39

bar toward him. I got up to the counter, grabbed a stool and sat down.

"We're closed," he said between his teeth.

"I know," I said. "I've just come in for the rest."

He didn't look at me but I could sense a faint tensing of his muscles. He had a hard, clear-minted face which looked red and raw with sun. He had the sort of complexion that doesn't tan very easily. His hair was very black; almost blue, it was so deep, and there wasn't a trace of grey in it.

He wore a red bow-tie with his midnight-blue jacket and the way the jacket bulged over his shoulders told me he had plenty of muscle there. He went on with his humming, pulled the plug out the sink and started drying the glasses with a red and green striped cloth.

"What you want, then? Apart from the rest?"

"Some information," I said.

He turned to look at me; he shrugged

and a wry expression passed across his face.

"About whom?"

"I'm looking for a girl," I said.

He shrugged again.

"Who isn't?"

"Save it," I said. "I've already had that line once today."

Unexpectedly, he grinned.

"You've been to see Dora."

"That's right," I said. "She sent me to you. Said you might be able to help."

He looked round the empty bar and lowered his voice.

"Information sometimes comes expensive."

"She told me that too."

He held one of the glasses out and admired his handiwork.

"I like to know who I'm talking to."

"Sure," I said.

I got out the copy of my licence and showed him. He looked at it with a heavy expression and didn't say anything.

"Who's the party?"

"A girl called Dale Holden," I said.

There was a wary look in the eyes now. I put down the photograph in front of him. He grunted approvingly.

"A looker."

"That's what Dora thought," I said.

He shook his head dubiously.

"I don't know. I might be able to help."

"Make up your mind," I said.

He looked at the picture and tapped it with a slightly damp forefinger.

"This could be trouble."

"That's my middle name," I said.

He grinned.

"All right, Mr Faraday. Can you come back tonight? Around eight o'clock? I might be able to dig something up by then."

"Fine," I said. "I'll be here."

I walked out and left him there, still polishing the glasses. I went down the staircase and out through the stale lobby smells of sweat and perfume. I drove on back across town thinking of a beautiful blonde chorine and the tiny figure of Jack Larsen sitting at his bar and whiling away his time playing his own fruit machines. It didn't make sense somehow. But then it seldom does in my racket.

I got outside a sandwich and a glass of beer at Jinty's. It wasn't as good as lunch but it was the best I could do at short notice. It was too late for me to pick up Stella at the office; she would have checked out by now. I'd probably get gas all afternoon.

I sighed. If I spent much time looking around spots for Dale Holden I'd be missing out on a lot of lunches and getting a lot of gassy stomachs. But for what Jack Larsen was willing to pay I could stand it if my stomach could.

I went over in a booth and studied the picture again. When the barman brought my second sandwich I showed it to him. He was a middle-aged, ex-baseball player with cropped hair, who wore a crumpled white jacket that looked as though he'd slept in it. He'd been around quite a while. Almost as long as I had which was saying something.

"Very nice," he said approvingly, shaking his head.

I sighed again.

"You missed the point," I told him. "Have you seen her around?"

He stared at me.

"You kidding, Mr Faraday? If I'd seen her first no-one else would have gotten a look in."

"Thanks for all the information," I said.

I put the picture away.

"You're welcome," he said brightly.

He came back to the table.

"If she comes around I'll tell her you're looking for her."

"You do that," I told him.

He beamed uncomprehendingly and went away. He must have lived a pretty simple life. I finished up my sandwich, ordered another beer and killed the lunch-hour.

By the time I got to the office the gas-pains were beginning nicely.

4

IT was around four o'clock when the phone buzzed. Stella had gone out to do some shopping for a few minutes and I was alone so I took it.

"Mr Faraday?"

The voice had a familiar ring. I admitted it.

"This is Dexter here, Mr Faraday. We were talking earlier in the day."

"Sure," I said. "What's the trouble?"

"No trouble," he said. "I got some time off. Could you come over to my apartment around eight instead of the bar. It's more private."

"Sure," I said. "How did you make out?"

"I dug something up for you," he said cautiously.

I took down the address he gave me.

"I'll be there," I said.

I put the phone down and sat staring at

the cracks in the ceiling. The smoke from my cigarette went up in an unwavering blue line. I got up then and switched the fan on. I sat down again while it redistributed the tired air. Like always the air-conditioning in our building wasn't working.

I finished the cigarette and stubbed it out in the earthenware tray on my desk. I reached for my scratchpad and scribbled a note for Stella. I frowned down at the stalled traffic on the boulevard, not noticing the mass of simmering metal; the miasma of gasoline fumes rising from the baking tarmac; and the smog that tied the whole thing together and gave it its charm.

I got up and went over to Stella's desk. I found the L.A. Directory and the section I wanted and carted it back over to my broadtop. I found Donald Laidlaw's number, wrote it on my blotter and carried the phone book back. I was already in a lather of sweat by the time I'd done that. I dialled Don's number.

He ran a talent agency specializing

in acts and singles for musical films; I wouldn't have thought there would have been much call for that these days with the closing of the big studios but he seemed to make a decent living at it. He'd gotten into cabaret and night-spot acts; and I understood he also supplied a lot of talent for nightclub scenes in TV films, particularly those turned at Universal. I hadn't thought of him until now.

I guessed be might have gone home or maybe out of town but I was lucky today; his secretary said he was in and what was more, would speak to me.

"It's been a long time, Mike."

"Sure," I said. "All of eight months, remember?"

"Ah, well," Laidlaw said. "Eight months out here on the coast is more like eight years compared to New York."

"I'll take L.A.," I said. "I'd like a little information, if you can spare a minute."

"Fire away," he said.

He had a big, booming voice and I could hold the receiver three feet away from my ear and still hear what he was saying. But he was a genuine character which was unusual in a town full of phoney bastards; especially in his profession.

"There's a girl called Dale Holden," I said. "Blonde, good-looker, about six feet tall. I've got a picture if you want it."

"Shouldn't be necessary," Laidlaw said lazily. "If she's on our books the name will be sufficient. Is it her real one?"

"Stage name," I said. "She's gone missing. Her father's a little worried."

"All right, Mike," Laidlaw said. "I know you can't go into detail. And you couldn't break down and tell me the girl's real name."

I grinned.

"You got it, Don. Ethics and all that stuff."

Laidlaw chuckled.

"Give me half an hour. I'll ring you back."

I thanked him and put the receiver down. I looked at the list Jack Larsen

48

had given me. Laidlaw's was about the only agency that wasn't on it. Which was curious. Because they were the major people in the field. Of course, Jack Larsen might or might not have known that. And the girl might be strictly small-time. Laidlaw wouldn't handle just anyone.

I sat there for what seemed like a long time. I went out to the waiting room and snubbed the door-catch, locking it. It gave me something to do. Besides, I didn't figure anything else would be happening this afternoon. And Stella had her own key anyway. Though I'd told her to go on home if she wanted. She was well up on the filing. It was one of those days.

I put my feet up on the desk and looked at my package of cigarettes. I had only three left. I frowned. I decided to save them for later. I closed my eyes, gave my pupils a rest. I sat like that for around ten minutes. Then I went over to the water cooler and poured myself a plastic cup of ice-cold. I drank that, rinsed the back of my neck in the wash-basin in the alcove and felt as hot as ever.

The phone buzzed just then. I got over to it as quickly as I could without melting my underwear. It was Laidlaw.

"We checked pretty thoroughly, Mike. She isn't one of ours. And I made one or two more calls. She must be pretty small-time if she operates around the city. We'd have heard of her otherwise. You sure you got the right name?"

"I'm sure," I said. "Thanks, Don, anyway. If you ever need a favour."

"I know where to go," Laidlaw said. "See you."

The phone clicked and went silent. I put it down in the cradle and sighed. I looked over to the window. I was alone with the smog and a dead bluebottle. I gave it up. I put on my coat and went out for a beer.

The address Dexter had given me was a bungalow not far from the beach. It took me an hour to get over there and I was a little late by the time I tooled the

Buick on to the private drive and cut the motor. There was a fine powdering of stars tonight and a big orange moon gilded the ocean and was broken into a million fragments of amber light. There was a nice breeze coming off the sea and I stood and enjoyed it for a moment or two, idly watching the chain of lights on a house-boat moored alongside a jetty half a mile down.

I wondered how a guy like Dexter could afford a seafront location. It was obvious he didn't make his living bar-tending; or rather he made his living through it. He evidently had a number of side-lines going. I wondered how much he'd bite me for. Though Jack Larsen was picking up the tab. The bungalow was a big timber building on brick foundations and with white-painted walls that extended up for about four feet until the cedar cladding took over.

There were lights on in two of the windows and the sound of a Mozart horn composition coming from a radio or a hi-fi outfit. I raised my eyebrows.

51

We got some class here, Faraday, I told myself. I went back to the gate-post and checked on the number. It was the place I wanted all right. I walked on up the cement drive, past a carved wooden statue of a naked boy holding a set of Pan-pipes to his lips. The eyes looked at me glassily as I went by. The thing was as phoney and passé as an old speech by Calvin Coolidge.

I felt the shirt sticking to my back again before I got to the porch. I was evidently expected because I saw one of the lights in rear go off. Then a brass lantern over the porch winked into life. By its light I could see a big white cat sitting on the stoop holding a live mouse between its claws. It looked at me solemnly and the mouse got up and made its escape. The cat looked at me reproachfully.

"Stupid," I said. "You and me both."

I reached down and scratched behind its ear. The animal reminded me of me. We both had prizes within our grasp and let them go. It was happening in my case all the time. There was a rattle at the door before I could get to the buzzer. Dexter opened it. He wore a tartan-check shirt, blue cotton slacks and white sneakers. His face was in the shadow.

"Right on the button, Mr Faraday," he said.

"You must have been watching out for me," I said.

Dexter grunted. He led the way into the hall and closed the door behind me.

"I heard your automobile. I'm pretty accurate at estimating how long it takes a person to walk up the drive if they park outside the gate."

"You have a lot of hobbies," I said. "And you must have pretty good hearing too."

"What's that?" Dexter said sharply.

We were standing in the hall now, which was dimly lit by the light spilling in through the living room door beyond so I still couldn't see his face properly.

"Hearing," I said. "If you could catch the sound of my motor over the noise of that hi-fi."

The Mozart was still jig-jogging majestically away. Dexter gave a short laugh.

"I was just boasting, Mr Faraday. I saw your headlights pass the gate as I was looking out the window just now."

"It's not important," I said.

I waited for Dexter to go ahead of me into the living room. He stood aside in the door but I didn't move so he had to precede me into the room. He went over to the fireplace and cut the hi-fi. The silence crawled back in again. I looked around. It was a pretty nice place.

Phoney, of course, like much of Californian house design. White-washed walls; oak beams; lots of brass gleaming under the light of the shaded lamps; an Olde Englishe Bar with Tudor-style chairs lined up along it. Phoney as hell but real, if you know what I mean. It was genuine oak; genuine furniture; but it looked out of place here, all thrown together like a designer dressing a film set. And it would have been expensive too.

Nothing comes cheap these days but this sort of set-up looked way beyond Dexter's class; I wondered if he'd borrowed the house for a month or two. Or maybe the evening. It was worth thinking about. Because if that were so it would open up a lot of interesting questions. I glanced around again as Dexter came back from the big stone fireplace that would have looked all right in an English baronial hall. The people who hang around outside Schwab's drugstore would have liked it.

"Bourbon all right?" he said with a wink.

"I'd prefer something long and cold with no alcoholic content right now, if it's all the same to you," I said. "Like lime-juice with ice."

He shrugged.

"It don't bother me none."

There was perspiration standing out on his forehead; I looked at him for a long moment. It might have been the heat of the evening; or again, it might have been something else. The living

55

room door was standing ajar. That led to the hall we'd just come in from. I went over and shut it. Dexter turned from the bar, the lip of the bottle clinking on the rim of the glass. He seemed jittery all right.

"Draught," I said.

I could see from his eyes he didn't believe me. Not that it mattered a damn to me what he believed. I went and sat down on a copy of a Knole settee.

"So you got the information," I said.

"I got some information," he corrected me.

I looked across to the far end of the room. There was another door there. That was ajar too.

I padded on over to it. Dexter watched me without saying anything. There was a bedroom beyond; the bed was unmade. There was a smell of stale cigarette smoke in there. I went back to the bar. Dexter reached for one of the big stools and hooked it over toward me with the toe of his shoe.

He put the long iced drink down on

the bar-counter just within my reach. I sat on the stool and leaned against the edge of the bar-counter and watched him. There was still something didn't sit quite right but I couldn't place it. Dexter seemed definitely ill at ease for a character who was used to mixing with people of every class and type. His hand shook ever so slightly as he mixed his own drink. He splashed the Scotch into the glass and added a cube of ice with silver tongs.

"Cheers," he said, raising the glass, not looking at me.

I raised my own glass and sipped it tentatively. It was all right. I sat and watched him while he got another stool and sat down opposite me.

"I haven't got much time," I said. "And no doubt you're a busy man too. You said you had some information to sell."

He raised a protesting finger.

"Easy, Mr Faraday. We're not in that much of a hurry. And there's a protocol to be observed."

"How much is it likely to cost me?"
I said.

He shrugged and put down his drink
on the bar-counter.

"Three hundred dollars."

I stared at him for a long moment.

"It had better be good information for
that money."

Dexter looked at me levelly.

"It's genuine," he said.

I nodded. I picked up my drink
again.

"All right, let's have it," I said.

He stared at me uncomfortably; little
red spots were beginning to start out on
his cheeks.

"It's usually cash on the nail," he said.

I grinned.

"We're having a little different pro-
cedure this time," I said. "Information
first. Then the cash, if I think it's
worth it."

Dexter made as if to get up, then
thought better of it.

"How do I know you're levelling?" he
said sullenly.

"You got my word for it," I said. "You'll get the money all right. But only when I'm satisfied."

Dexter drew down the corners of his mouth.

"The girl," he said. "She isn't Larsen's daughter."

I sat very still and focused my gaze on his slightly shaking hands which were cupped round the base of his glass. The room seemed to have grown very close and sticky.

"How do you make that out?" I said.

Dexter made an irritated clucking noise with his tongue.

"Because I got the right information," he said. "That's what you're paying for. She's his girl-friend."

My incredulity must have shown on my face because Dexter shifted uncomfortably on the stool and put his hands out, palms upward.

"Believe me or not, Mr Faraday, but you can't buck the facts. I got proof."

"I believe you," I said. "I have to play things by the book. If the client tells me it's his daughter, I accept the fact."

Dexter put his hand round the stem of his glass again.

"Sure," he said placatingly. "We all make mistakes."

"I don't see the point," I said. "It wouldn't have made any difference. His girl-friend, his wife. She's disappeared. It's all the same to me."

Dexter put his hand out.

"That worth three hundred dollars?"

I shook my head.

"Nowhere near, sonny. I want to know where she is. I was told you could probably help."

Dexter showed his gums in an unpleasant manner. He reached over the other side of the bar with an unmistakable gesture. I started to get off the stool, balling my fist to re-arrange his bridge-work. I didn't make it.

A character as big as a house rose up from behind the bar and hit me over the head with a blackjack. It felt like a ten-ton beer truck. I lost all interest after that.

5

I COUGHED as water ran down my face. The room was coming into focus nicely.

"He must have a skull like concrete," said Dexter admiringly.

He stood over me, grinning. I could see more clearly now. He had my wallet in his hand.

"I think we said three hundred, Mr Faraday. Just so you can see it's all above board."

He peeled off the bills and put them in his pocket. He put the wallet down on the bar-counter.

"I shall want a receipt for that," I said.

Dexter smiled. I was sitting on the Knole settee which had been dragged over near the bar. I looked at the long glass that was still standing on the bar-top. I could only have been out a few minutes.

61

"I could use that drink now," I said.

A hand as big as a ham-bone came out the shadows, picked up the drink and threw it over me. It felt refreshing.

"Thanks," I said. "I needed that."

I looked at Dexter for a long moment.

"Don't let me catch you around town."

Dexter looked uneasy.

"You may not be around yourself," he said uncomfortably.

A massive head came forward into the lamplight. The jaw jerked toward Dexter in an unmistakable gesture. He swallowed and went out quickly. I heard his footsteps going away down the concrete path outside. A few seconds later a car whispered away in the darkness.

"Rented like I thought," I said. I meant the house, of course.

The back of my head was beginning to throb nicely. The big man eased forward on the bar stool and looked at me impassively.

"Now, Mr Faraday, it looks like you've some explaining to do."

"That's my line," I said.

The big man shook his head. I could see him clearly for the first time. He had on a white tropical suit worn over an open-neck cream silk shirt. He was about seven feet tall and proportionately broad. He was around thirty and in top condition. I shifted on the settee and got into a more comfortable position. He kept on looking at me and waited for me to speak.

He had a frank, open face; wide brown eyes and a mouth that wasn't unhumorous. The strangest thing about him was his hair; it clung in small curls all over his scalp. Nothing unusual in that but the hair itself was snow-white. It gave him a frosty look every time he moved and the light caught it.

"I'm waiting, Mr Faraday."

"I don't know what you expect me to say," I said. "If you know my name you also obviously know that I'm a private eye hired by Jack Larsen to find his daughter. She's a girl called Dale Holden. Just now Dexter said she wasn't Larsen's daughter. That make sense to you?"

The giant momentarily closed his eyes like he was in pain.

"It makes sense all right, Mr Faraday," he said. "Which puts you on the other side. Anyone working for Jack Larsen is automatically blacked in my book."

"Just a minute," I said. "Just where do you come in all this?"

The giant looked at me patiently as though I'd just asked him the dumbest question.

"She's my sister," he said simply.

I started to get up, found my legs would hardly hold me. The big man made a menacing movement with his massive fist.

"Try anything I'll take you apart."

"Sure you could," I said. "But I'm in no condition to give you any competition."

I clawed my way to the bar, stood staring at him. He would have been a nice-looking character if the anger hadn't showed in every pore.

"I just want a drink," I said. "One that goes down the throat and not on the suit."

He stared at me open-mouthed. Then he grunted.

"You're a cool one, Mr Faraday. Sit down. I'll get you the drink."

"What I had before," I said. "A fruit juice with ice."

I sat down on the settee again until he silently padded round the end of the bar and put the cold glass in my hand. Holden, if that was his name, went back and sat up on the bar stool and looked at me with hard, questioning eyes. I raised the glass and eased the lime-juice down my throat. It was as cold as a mountain stream. Some of the throbbing seemed to lift from my head. For tonight it was the best drink I'd ever tasted.

"Larsen's a crook," Holden said suddenly.

"I don't work for crooks," I said.

The big man laughed hoarsely.

"Since when did private dicks get so particular?"

I looked at him across the rim of the glass.

"Since way back in my case," I said.

"And if Larsen's a crook, what's your sister doing knocking around with him?"

The big man poised himself on the stool, raising his balled fist. I got ready to throw my glass in his face. It wasn't necessary. He eased back on the stool with a black scowl.

"Don't try my temper again, mister."

"It's easy to say that. It doesn't take much to sap anybody from behind a bar," I said.

The big man broke out an uneasy smile. It lightened his face.

"That was no sap," he said. "I just used the back of my hand."

I felt the base of my skull.

"You could have fooled me," I said. "What is all this about your sister?"

Holden shook his head angrily; he fastened his paw around the glass on the counter in front of him and got some more of it down him.

"You're working for Larsen. You tell me."

I shook my head.

"I'm a new boy on the case, Mr

Holden. Larsen asked to see me. He said his daughter ran away from home three weeks ago. He gave me her photograph and asked if I could trace her. I said I'd try. That brings Dexter in."

The big man put his glass down on the bar-top with a tinkle of ice. His brow was corrugated with thought.

"I'd like to believe you, Mr Faraday."

I grinned.

"I don't give a damn what you believe. You know I could have you arrested for assault."

Holden shrugged. He had a resentful look on his face.

"Go ahead. See where it will get you," he said defiantly.

I shook my head.

"I don't operate like that. After all, what's a tap here and there between friends. I'm looking for your sister. You're obviously looking for her too. I'd say we ought to join forces and see what we come up with. You evidently know more about Larsen than I do."

Holden had a startled look on his

67

face. He swallowed hard once or twice like he couldn't believe what he was hearing.

"Well I'll be damned," he told his drink.

He looked at me sharply and some of the suspicion had lifted from his face.

"You're a cool one, Mr Faraday, and no mistake. Only private dicks I've ever dealt with were greasy little men who hid under beds, bribed chambermaids and sold out their mothers for a couple of bucks."

I finished off the lime-juice and held out my empty glass for another.

"You've been seeing too many old Warner Brothers movies," I told him. "We do things differently today."

Holden got up and took my glass; the initiative had passed to me now but I knew he could still be dangerous if I made any false moves. He came back and put the cool glass into my hand. He went and leaned against the bar, frowning into his own drink.

"All right, Mr Faraday," he said at

last. "Suppose I do play ball? What's your proposition?"

The bar was full of smoke. I lit my third cigarette and squinted at Holden through the haze. The big man sat now at the end of the copy of the Knole settee. More relaxed, he was quite amiable when he wasn't hitting me over the head or using his fist as a croquet mallet. His open cream shirt revealed his thick neck muscles.

"You should have carried a gun, Mr Faraday," he said simply.

"I do normally," I told him. "But not on this type of case."

He shook his head.

"If Jack Larsen's involved you're going to need a gun sooner or later."

"You seem to know a lot about him," I said.

"Enough."

Holden drained his glass gloomily and looked at me. This time I got up and went over to the bar and refilled it for him. I came back and sat down on the other end of the settee to face him.

"Let's see how far we've got," I said. "You're George Holden. You're Dale Holden's brother. She ran away from home in San Francisco two years ago. You came to L.A. to find her. You knew she was working as a dancer because your mother got a postcard from time to time."

"I heard tell of her here and there." He shook his head in disbelief.

"We was real close only two-three years ago, Mr Faraday. I don't know how things got to this stage."

"People grow up," I said. "They change."

The big man stared into the bottom of his glass.

"Some things don't change," he said stubbornly. "Real close, even for brother and sister."

"But you managed to trace her?"

"She was working in the chorus line in this cheap dance palace," he said. "She was already tied up with Larsen. He had some idea of making her a big star. You know the drivel."

He gave a short, barking laugh.

Course, I didn't know all that then. Dale seemed changed a hell of a lot. Not glad to see me at all. She said she'd write. She never did. When I called around she'd pulled out."

"And no forwarding address," I said.

George Holden shook his head.

"But there was a character in the show Dale had been quite keen on. I beat the truth out of him. He told me where Dale had gone."

"So you went to see Jack Larsen?"

George Holden chuckled again.

"God, I was green. I didn't know anything about the guy. He was pretty nice at first. Even let me see Dale. I thought she was high on drink. I guessed later it might have been drugs. She didn't even recognise me."

He paused and took a stiff swill at his glass.

"Next time I came around I was thrown out."

He looked at me with satisfaction.

71

"Took six of them to do it. I came back with the police. That didn't do no good. Next time I showed they had guards and dogs."

I was silent for a moment.

"What do you think Larsen's up to?"

Holden shrugged.

"He's a big-time racketeer, I guess. That's why I figured you for a rotten apple too. Any guy that would work for a character like that. Guess I owe you an apology."

He held out his hand impulsively. I took it, felt my finger-bones creak in his crushing grip.

"Just make sure next time," I said. "Dexter put the bite on you when I came around?"

Holden's face was sombre.

"I paid him three hundred too."

"I aim to get mine back," I said. "I don't like being used by creeps like Dexter. You want yours?"

Holden shook his head again.

"Put it down to experience. You going back to see that crooked dwarf? Jesus, when I think of that creep and a girl like Dale . . . "

He broke off; his big hands were clenched round the glass so tightly I thought it would splinter in his fingers.

"I'll have a word with Jack Larsen," I said. "But if he's looking for your sister too, he might be in the clear."

"Don't bank on it," Holden said.

"What have you got against him?" I said.

Holden shrugged.

"Dale for one thing. For another, if he had nothing to hide why did he have me thrown off?"

"Perhaps he figured you were trespassing," I said mildly.

Holden's face flushed a dull mahogany colour.

"You don't know him like I do, Mr Faraday," he said.

He was silent for a moment, his big paw absently stroking his glass like it was a cat and gaining pleasure from the motion.

"Seems I may have been wrong about

you, Mr Faraday," he said grudgingly.

"No need to apologize," I said. "You already did that."

"I got a proposition for you," he went on as though he hadn't heard. I sighed. It was something I'd come across before.

"I know," I said. "You want to retain my services."

The big man looked surprised.

"What's wrong with that?"

"Everything," I said. "Firstly, I already got a client. Secondly, I can't take money from two clients simultaneously on the same case."

I gave him a long, hard look.

"Especially if they've got clashing interests."

Holden looked disappointed. He gulped fiercely at his drink as though I'd just insulted him.

"I tell you what I can do," I said. "I'll keep a watching brief and play it by ear."

"What does that mean?" Holden grumbled.

"Well, if I learn anything and it

won't actually harm Larsen but the information might benefit you, I'll keep you informed," I said.

"I'm not quite sure I understood that, but I'll accept your offer," Holden grinned.

"Sure," I said. "Particularly as it won't cost you a penny."

"You're all right. Mr Faraday," Holden said solemnly.

"I could have told you that before I came in," I said fingering my scalp.

6

I GOT out the Buick, locked the door and walked up toward the entrance. I could hear the noise the band was making two hundred yards away. I hadn't been able to get Holden's address out of him. He wouldn't give it me and I was in no condition to beat it out of him. If I was going to meet people his size on Jack Larsen's case I was going to carry the Smith-Wesson from now on in.

In the end I gave Holden one of my business cards and told him to contact me in a day or two; I figured he'd be around soon enough if he wanted any news of the girl. Not that I was likely to have it. The more I looked at it the more I figured the case was going to be a complicated one. The simple ones always are. And nothing more simple than tracing a girl's address.

A fat man came out the main doors

as I got up the steps. He had a round, red face shiny with sweat and a nasty little black mustache that sat under his nostrils like a dead vole. He obviously had a lot under his belt and he missed two steps in three. He wore a black fedora with his black dinner suit and he raised it graciously as I got up near him.

Unfortunately he missed his footing again and would have come down on his face if I hadn't got to him in time. I lowered him to the treads without breaking the backs of either of us. His breath came up hot and reeking in my face.

"Thank you, sir," he said with old-world courtesy. "These steps seem to get bigger as the evening goes on."

"It's something I've noticed," I said.

I got my hands under his armpits and tried to jack him up. He was too heavy for me. I gave it up for the moment.

"Every health and happiness to you, sir," he burbled.

"And may Allah be with you," I said, entering into the spirit of the thing.

The fat man beamed foolishly as though I'd done him a favour.

"That's awfully clean-limbed of you, sir," he said.

A commissionaire in gold braid was hot-footing it down the steps to us by this time. He shook his head sorrowfully.

"I warned you, Mr Cartwright," he said. "You're in no fit condition, sir."

"I feel great," the fat man said.

The commissionaire gave me a frosty look, like it was my fault.

"That's just the trouble, sir."

He bent down and hooked the fat man up with surprising ease; it was a remarkable performance. But then I guessed he'd had a lot of practice. He turned a worried face to me.

"It was decent of you to help, sir. Mr Cartwright is one of our most valued customers.

"So it seems," I said.

"He really oughtn't to drive this evening," the commissionaire said.

I gave him a hard look.

"I'm astonished that anyone in their

78

senses should suggest it," I said.

The commissionaire shrugged apologetically. The fat man almost slid to the ground again.

"You don't know Mr Cartwright, sir."

"Evidently not," I said. "Hard man to stop is he?"

The commissionaire nodded.

"Very hard indeed, sir."

I looked at the fat man, swaying foolishly in the commissionaire's grasp.

"Well, he's your problem," I said. "Don't strike a match near him or you'll both go up."

The commissionaire wore a pained expression. He turned away, guiding the fat man down the steps.

"Thank you again, sir," the fat man said. "Every health and happiness to you."

He twisted round and looked at me with bleary eyes.

"We must have a drink together some time."

I tried not to inhale the fumes too deeply.

"We just did," I said.

I went on up the steps and left them to it. The muzak was off tonight but otherwise the chocolate brown and gold of the lobby of The Crazy Horse looked almost as tawdry as when I'd been there in daylight. There was one main difference in the atmosphere; the smells of stale sweat and cigarette smoke were overlaid with the cheap perfume the cleaners had sprayed the place out with.

The blare of the live band on the rostrum in the big restaurant beyond the far doors made one forget the decor. A couple came out while I was there and the amplified blare seemed to lift the roof. No-one else appeared to notice. I sighed. You're getting old, Faraday, I told myself. You can't take it any more at thirty-three. I say that at least twice on every case so I didn't take it too seriously this time.

The Smith-Wesson .38 in its nylon holster pressed against my shoulder muscles as I went on over to the staircase with the gold lettering MEZZANINE

BAR over it. I'd decided I'd had enough fooling around with characters like George Holden; fists were no good against people built like ten-ton trucks and with hands like hydraulic rams. Not unless one had the get up and go of John Wayne; the durability of Steve Reeves; and the build of Primo Carnera. I didn't kid myself. I wasn't in that league.

So I'd broken out the heavy artillery from the cupboard I use as an armoury in the bedroom of my rented house over on Park West. I might need it if I went back to Jack Larsen's. The gateman alone would have rated Ernest Borgnine-type casting in the meanest Western. And this wasn't Hollywood. It was reality. I went up the stairs three at a time. Again a waiter was already halfway down the main flight. It even looked like the same one I'd met before.

"Dexter in?" I said.

He stared at me indifferently. It was a small world all right. It was the same waiter.

"You're in a rut, mister," he said sadly.

"He's just checking the bar takings."

I grinned.

"Looks like I came at the right time."

The character in the midnight-blue jacket shook his head sombrely.

"You don't know The Crazy Horse, mister. There ain't no right time for a dump like this."

I went on in the Mezzanine Bar, pushing aside the iron rococo door I remembered from my last visit. The place was blue with smoke; there were about twenty people in and the air was heavy with dull, half-sodden conversations. There was a youngster with black glossy hair going around waiting on table. Dexter was up the far end, the till open, busy with calculations. I eased on down, my footsteps inaudible on the thick carpeting.

Dexter didn't see me coming. These characters never look at people's faces. They're just orders so far as they're concerned. He kept on totting up figures, licking a pencil-stub with a very blue tongue. I wondered how much he was going to allow the management out of the take. I stopped in front of him.

"What's your pleasure, sir?"

He still had the cigarette jammed in the corner of his mouth.

"I'll have my three hundred bucks," I said.

He opened his eyes wide then, his mouth a black O in the middle of his face. The cigarette fell on the bar-top in a shower of sparks. He reached under the counter with a quick grabbing movement. I hit him with all my strength then; my knuckles connected with his mouth, making a satisfying click. He flew upward like a rocket, crashing heavily against the bottles in back of the bar.

His eyes glazed and there was the tinkle of broken glass somewhere in rear; no-one moved. The conversation just stopped and I saw the boy with dark hair lifting a glass, his gesture frozen in mid-air. I stepped around the end of the bar quickly. Dexter was completing his slide to the floor. I rummaged around in his pocket, found his wallet. I fanned out three hundred bucks from the bundle, shoved the rest of the wad back in his top pocket.

A big man in evening dress came in through a door alongside the bar. There were dark red spots showing on his cheeks.

"What's the trouble, buddy?"

"No trouble," I said, tapping my breast pocket. "Just collecting a debt from a welsher."

I pointed to the bundle of notes.

"If you're the manager, I'd have the bar takings checked."

The big man's eyes were like gimlets. He stood back, not interfering.

"Thanks for the advice."

"You're welcome," I said.

I put the notes in my pocket. Dexter was coming round now. He groaned and blood ran out the corner of his mouth. His eyes focused up on me.

"I'll get the police in," he said thickly.

"Sure," I said. "Sue me."

I walked on out without looking at anybody. Nobody made a move to stop me. I got out through the front entrance and found the Buick. I was still smiling as I drove away.

"You were a chump," Stella said.

"You knew that anyway," I told her.

There was a fine rain falling outside; it had surprised me as well as the weather forecasters. I was taking an afternoon off from the case today. I'd spent the morning tramping round theatrical agencies. No-one seemed to have heard of the Holden number. Which wasn't surprising; she seemed to move in strictly non-Frank Sinatra circles. Stella hadn't come up with anything either.

She was wearing tartan trews todays with a pale blue shirt that looked sensational over her superstructure. She wore a belt made of beaten gold hooplets that glistened as she walked and drew in her flat stomach even flatter. I could have watched it all day. Especially as it was cooler with the rain.

Stella stopped her note-taking and looked at me pityingly; the gold bell of her hair shimmered in the light of the lamps.

"You did well to recover your money, Mike," she said. "But you were dumb over Dexter and Holden."

She'd said it so often it was beginning to sound like a comedy double act; one that would have fitted in on the same bill as Larsen's Dancing Daughter.

I set fire to a cigarette and frowned at the cracks in the ceiling.

"It wasn't my money, it was Larsen's," I said. "Isn't it about coffee time?"

Stella smiled.

"Every time is coffee time with you," she said.

She got up and went over to the alcove and switched on the percolator. I sat on frowning at the rain blearing the window pane and rinsing the smog down the glass in dark streaks so that the drowned cars on the boulevard beyond looked like they were struggling through glue.

Stella came back and sat down on the edge of her desk. She folded her arms across her breasts and looked at me appraisingly, waiting for the coffee to brew.

"You're going to see Jack Larsen again?"

"Sure," I said. "And ask him what's the idea."

"Does it matter if you're on his payroll?" Stella said.

"Now who's being cynical?" I said. "Sure it matters. It matters to me, it matters to the whole business. If the client's a crook or not telling the truth it make one hell of a difference."

"I was only kidding, Mike," Stella said.

"I'll maybe look over there in the morning," I said. "It doesn't matter to me whether the Holden girl's his daughter or his fancy woman. Only I'd like to get it straight and not hear it from other people."

Stella went over and busied herself with cups and saucers. She put her head round the screen again.

"You didn't say how Dexter got on to Holden," she said.

87

"He didn't say and I didn't ask," I said.

I grinned at Stella's expression; she looked quite shocked. I waited until she'd brought the coffee over and put it down on my blotter; she went over to her desk, pushed her typewriter back and sifted sugar into her own cup.

"Biscuits in the tin," she said.

I looked around the desk.

"No tin," I said.

I went over ponderously, got the tin and came back. Stella raised her eyes to the ceiling.

"Some hardship," she told the filing cabinet.

I grinned. I shifted gear on a chocolate nut fudge delight, picked out a couple of others and took the tin over to Stella. I went back to my swivel chair and concentrated on the best part of the day.

"Maybe Holden found Dexter the same way I did," I said. "Or maybe Dexter already knew Holden was looking for his sister. He bit the big guy for the same amount."

"At least you got a rebate," Stella said.

"Anyway it was a memorable meeting," I said. "A sort of landmark in showbiz."

"You can say that again," Stella said.

We sat drinking coffee and nibbling at the biscuits. I'd had my second cup and presently Stella went back to hitting her typewriter keys again. I signed a couple of cheques for her, read the two letters she'd put on my blotter and signed those too. That seemed about it for the afternoon. I read the *Examiner* for half an hour or so and by then it was about time to quit.

"You might as well knock it off, honey," I said. "There won't be anyone else around this time of day."

Stella sheathed her typewriter, paused a moment, her head on one side as she looked at me.

"You sure you can handle it if someone does?"

I looked at her in surprise.

"I even tie my own shoe-laces now," I said.

Stella chuckled.

"You'd get jumped on twice as hard if I wasn't around."

"Meaning what?" I said.

Stella jerked her thumb over toward the frosted glass of the waiting room door.

"Meaning there's been someone in the waiting room for the past couple of minutes."

I frowned at her.

"I took the buzzer off. I suppose you forgot to put it back on?"

Stella looked at me with a pitying expression.

"As you didn't tell me you'd disconnected it, there was no question of me forgetting," she said primly.

I sighed. She was right of course. But even if she hadn't been there was no way of winning. Not with Stella. I got up from the desk. I went over toward the waiting room door. A dark shadow moved across the pane. I looked warningly at Stella. She got back in against the wall. She's a girl who never needs telling twice where business is concerned. She's a real pro in that respect.

I opened up the door. The tall, thin man standing just outside blinked mildly at me. He still wore the midnight-blue suit. The glossy dark hair shone above the deep tan. I stepped back and beckoned him into the room.

"I don't like people who creep around behind the furniture," I said. "Come on in, Mr Lauritzen."

7

GREG LAURITZEN bit back an angry retort. He remembered his manners in time and made a half-bow to Stella who'd sat down again.

"We didn't finish our conversation yesterday, Mr Faraday," he said uneasily. "So I thought I'd come on over."

"I'm glad you did," I said. "There are one or two things I'd like to get straight about Mr Larsen."

Lauritzen shot me a quick glance.

"I thought you'd get wise to him, Mr Faraday," he said smoothly. "You've found out Miss Holden isn't his daughter."

"That and some other things," I said. "I thought you didn't know what he wanted to see me about."

Lauritzen sank into the chair in front of my desk and looked from me to Stella and then back to me again.

"I guessed," he said. "But you'd have found that out straight away if you hadn't been in such a hurry to leave."

"Maybe it was a tactical indiscretion," I said. "But you're here now. What is it you want to tell me?"

Lauritzen glanced nervously at Stella and inclined his head in her direction.

"Is it really necessary to have the young lady present? This is a matter of some discretion."

"I trust her more than I would myself," I said. "She stays. Otherwise you go."

Lauritzen swallowed once or twice like his dialogue was about to choke him. Stella looked at me with very bright eyes. She blew me a kiss over Lauritzen's shoulder.

"Don't get me wrong, Mr Faraday," Lauritzen eventually-croaked. "I wasn't implying anything . . ."

"I'm sure you weren't," I told him. "Consider us like you would a monastery. With myself as the gardener and this young lady as the Mother Superior."

Stella almost laughed outright but she

managed to control her features in time. Lauritzen's face turned a nasty shade of puce but he also managed to control himself.

"Very amusing, Mr Faraday," he said softly. "But I take your point."

"Would you like some coffee?" I said. "Stella makes the very best."

Lauritzen shot a glance over his shoulder at Stella.

"That's extremely agreeable, Mr Faraday. I'll take you up on it."

Stella raised her eyes to the ceiling.

"You just had some, Mike."

I grinned.

"This is for Mr Lauritzen, honey."

Stella got up with a slow smile.

"And if he's having some you'd like one as well," she said in her briskest voice. "Get it."

She went over to the alcove and I heard the snick of the percolator going on. It was the most used piece of equipment in the office today.

Lauritzen frowned at me and bent forward across the desk.

"You don't think she's offended at what I said?"

He jerked his thumb over toward Stella's profile on the frosted glass. I leaned back in my swivel chair and focused my eyes up somewhere beyond Lauritzen toward the cracks in the ceiling. I shook my head.

"Don't worry about it," I said. "It's nothing to do with the coffee. Just a private joke."

Lauritzen nodded like I'd said something important. Stella was back now. She went and fetched her notebook and gold pencil and sat at her own desk, the tip poised over the paper. Lauritzen glanced back over his shoulder.

"No notes, please," he said. "Not at this stage. I wouldn't like it to get back to Mr Larsen."

"I'll bet you wouldn't," I said. "You don't trust him and he doesn't trust you, right?"

Lauritzen shot me a startled look.

"That's about it," he said. "You catch on quickly."

"What beats me is why you stick together," I said.

Lauritzen grinned.

"The money's good," he said. "And he has to have somebody."

"That's two reasons," I said. "But neither very good from Jack Larsen's point of view."

Stella got up and went to bring the coffee. Lauritzen tried again.

"Look, Mr Faraday," he said. "I don't know why but apparently we got off on the wrong foot. I was just trying to put you wise to Jack Larsen. This girl, for instance?"

"I'm listening," I said. "What about her?"

Lauritzen shrugged. He glanced over his shoulder to make sure Stella wasn't within ear-shot.

"She was his fancy piece for a while. If you knew what I know, Mr Faraday. Movies, live displays, all that sort of stuff. What a creep. She went through it all."

"What for?" I said.

Lauritzen shrugged again. It was

something he was good at.

"Money. What else?"

He chuckled throatily.

"Sure as hell it wasn't for love of Jack Larsen. He's no Adonis."

"What about Larsen?" I said. "Was he fond of her?"

Lauritzen turned around to make sure Stella was still in the alcove.

"Perhaps," he said shortly. "It was difficult to tell. He certainly spent a lot of money on, her. She came to me once, a while back. She wanted out."

"So you helped her?" I said.

A fleeting expression of fear passed across Lauritzen's face.

"I tried," he said. "I gave her some money and a bus ticket."

"You were keen on her yourself," I said.

Lauritzen shook his head angrily. Dark red showed on his cheeks beneath the tan.

"You shouldn't have said that, Mr Faraday," he muttered.

"But it's true?" I said.

He shrugged again.

"You could say that," he said. "Yeah, Dale and I had been out a few times. She wasn't a hard girl to love."

"You'd better tell me about her," I said. "Because if you gave her a bus ticket . . ."

Lauritzen leaned forward and interrupted me.

"You got it wrong, Mr Faraday. Dale didn't use the ticket or the money. I found them both in her room after she disappeared."

"Disappeared?"

Lauritzen shook his head.

"Sure, disappeared," he said suddenly. "One evening she was there. The next instant it seemed, she'd gone. A lot of her stuff was still in the house."

I looked at Lauritzen for a long moment. He seemed sincere so far as this went.

"So what's your theory?"

The tall man turned slightly in his chair, watching the shadow of Stella on the frosted glass of the alcove, pouring the coffee.

"She and Jack had a quarrel," he said. "She'd wanted out for a long time. He stopped her having a career. I was hoping to set her up in something myself."

He turned burning eyes on me.

"Jack was insanely jealous. He would have done anything."

"What are you telling me?" I said.

Stella came back and put the coffee down on the desk in front of Lauritzen. She went back to the alcove for mine and her own.

"Jack has efficient ways of making people disappear," he said. "His heavy boys could have done it."

"Murder?" I said.

"It's been done before."

"It doesn't make sense," I said. "Not if he loved the girl."

"It could have been a sudden rage," Lauritzen said.

"That lets out the heavies, then," I told him. "It still doesn't make sense. Besides, why would he call me in? To implicate himself?"

Stella put down the coffee on my blotter and went over to her own desk and sat watching the two of us without saying anything. I stirred my cup, adding a mite more sugar.

Lauritzen clicked his teeth like he was annoyed.

"I'm just putting up some suggestions, Mr Faraday. Just throwing out a few lines of thought."

"Trouble is you're not throwing them out in the right direction," I said. "What about the brother? He tells me he's been shown the gate when he went up to see Larsen."

Lauritzen clicked his teeth like he was annoyed.

"Not when I was there. But that's another motive. The brother would naturally have a grudge. So maybe Larsen hired you to take the heat off himself."

I sat back and focused up on the cracks in the ceiling. Stella maintained a diplomatic silence, though I noticed she'd started taking notes.

"You wouldn't have a picture of the Holden girl?" I said. "One that looks something like her? That might enable me to trace her more easily."

Lauritzen looked surprised, as though the idea had never occurred to him.

"I got something in my wallet, Mr Faraday. But I'd want you to take good care of it."

"Sure," I said.

I waited while he got out the shot in the leather folder; it was a decent studio portrait and looked nothing like the thing Larsen had given me. The girl wore a tailored suit; the face had character as well as beauty. I could tell why two men as diverse as Larsen and Lauritzen would be fascinated. I passed the picture over to Stella.

"I'll get it copied," she said. "And let Mr Lauritzen have the original back."

"Personally," said Lauritzen quickly. "Not through the post."

His eyes roved around the office like he could see Jack Larsen sitting at the bar with his fruit machines, watching him. Lauritzen looked at me with sick eyes. I suddenly felt sorry for him.

"I suppose a retainer wouldn't help, Mr Faraday? I'd like you to act for me."

I shook my head.

"I couldn't do it. I'm already retained by Mr Larsen. But I'll keep my eyes and ears open. If I hear anything you'll be one of the first to know."

Lauritzen seemed awkward and almost pathetic.

"I'd certainly be grateful."

I put down my coffee cup and looked across at Stella.

"Anything else you want to tell me? You think some harm has come to Dale Holden."

Lauritzen shook his head gloomily.

"From what I know of her she'd have contacted me if she'd been able," he said.

I gave him a long, hard look.

"You know what that means?"

"Murder," Lauritzen said.

"Not only that," I told him. "Big trouble for everyone. I've got the brother on my back, too."

Lauritzen started to get up, stood fiddling around in front of the desk like he was anxious to get away but not quite sure he wanted to go.

"That's your problem, Mr Faraday."

I nodded. I sat back in my swivel chair and stared at him. Then I shifted my gaze on to Stella. The view was better in her direction.

"You'll let me know if you hear anything?"

"Sure, Mr Faraday."

"Or if you have any afterthoughts," I said.

"Meaning what?" Lauritzen said sharply.

"Meaning that you'd like to level with me," I said. "There's more to tell, isn't there?"

Lauritzen shifted his feet. All the ease and confidence I'd noted in him when I turned up at Larsen's place seemed to have disappeared. I couldn't imagine anyone like Jack Larsen hiring him as he appeared now.

"Maybe, Mr Faraday. When I get to know you better."

"Just keep in touch," I said. "I'll carry on rooting around."

Lauritzen went out so quietly we hardly heard the waiting room door close behind him.

8

"DALE HOLDEN must be quite a girl," Stella said.

She put her head on one side and looked at the photograph.

"If she's still alive," I said.

Stella gave me a quick look. Her eyes were serious now.

You think it's possible, Mike? She seems to have these fellows on a string."

"I think it's very likely, honey," I said. "With that sort of track record."

I looked over to where the neons were making jazzy patterns at the window.

"This case looks like being a lot of trouble," I said. "With all these characters on my back. Not forgetting the girl's brother."

Stella smiled sympathetically.

"But you made a thousand dollars out of it," she said. "So you come out on the credit side whatever happens."

"We'll see," I said. "Right now I could use a drink."

"A useful suggestion," Stella said. "And an excuse for spending more of Mr Larsen's money."

I grinned.

"There's a nice little wine bar I know. It's on the way home."

Stella got up and switched off the light over her desk. She stood looking at me reflectively. I got up off my butt and went over and switched off the fan. Not that it seemed to make much difference whether it was on or not. The air-conditioning we have seems to distribute hot air in summer and cold air in winter. Not that the winters are all that cold out here on the West Coast. But it's the principle.

I looked across at the window. It was raining now. I sighed. I went over to stand close to Stella in the semi-gloom. There was only the light from the waiting-room door coming in now.

"You know, honey, if it hadn't been for you I'd have given up years ago."

106

Stella smiled. I could see its brightness even in the gloom.

"That'll be the day," she said.

"It's true," I told her.

"It's just the weather, Mike," Stella said. "It's not like you to get sentimental."

"I'm not sentimental," I said. "I'm levelling."

"It's just the rain and the smog," Stella said. "You'll get over it."

I grinned. We were just moving over toward the door when the phone buzzed.

"That was your fault," Stella said. "If you hadn't stalled around we'd have been out of here."

"We could let it ring," I said.

Stella sighed this time. She went over and put on the room light. She lifted the phone.

"Faraday Investigations. Yes, just a moment. I'll put him on."

She turned to me, one hand over the receiver.

"It's Mr Larsen. I could say you're out . . ."

I grinned.

"After you just told him I was in."

I picked up the phone from my own desk.

"You must be psychic, Mr Larsen."

"How come?"

The voice still sounded like a buzz-saw going through sandstone. If I hadn't met him I'd have imagined him six feet tall.

"I was going to ring you," I said. "I'd like to come out in the morning."

"You've found something?"

The voice was quick and suspicious.

"You could say that, Mr Larsen. What were you ringing about?"

There was a long silence on the wire; so long that I was about to repeat the question. Then Larsen spoke again.

"I was naturally anxious . . . My daughter . . . "

"I think we can drop the daughter bit," I said.

There was another long silence.

"Oh, you found out?"

He didn't seem at all perturbed; there was no change from the normal in his tones. Leastways, what passed for normal in his voice.

"Naturally," I said. "Why didn't you level with me?"

"It's a long story, Mr Faraday."

The voice was weary now; it may have been my imagination but it sounded as though the edges were blurred by drink. Except he used only soft drinks.

"We'll discuss it tomorrow if you don't mind."

"I don't mind," I said. "It's your money. You're only buying your own time."

Larsen chuckled.

"You're frank at any rate."

"That's more than I can say for you, Mr Larsen," I said. "I'll be out tomorrow around ten o'clock."

I put the phone down without waiting for him to reply. Stella had stood with her own phone to her ear, her hand still over the mouthpiece. Now she put the instrument down with a faint click in the silence. She had a smile on her face.

"A bit brusque, weren't you? After all, it is his money."

"He won't get value for it if he doesn't level." I said.

I looked round at the office; despite all the rain outside, it was as hot as hell still. I went on over to the light-switch. Stella went out into the waiting room. I doused the lights and locked up. We rode down in the creaky elevator. The atmosphere was so close we were silent all the way to the street.

It was a bright morning with a little heat-haze on the hills and I forgot the smog and the gasoline-fumes as I drove on over to Larsen's place. I found the turning I was looking for and tooled the Buick over on to Ticonderoga Drive, the springs protesting at the ruts in the poor road surface. I changed down and idled on along the road, admiring the shadows of the palm-fronds across the Buick's bodywork.

I stopped near the entrance of the lane and idled the motor while I lit a cigarette. I flipped the spent match-stalk among the dusty rocks at the roadside and feathered blue smoke out through my nostrils. I watched a big, heavy-winged bird soaring and gliding above the canyon. He was using the currents of hot air to get lift and was going up faster than an express elevator. I admired his progress for a while until he disappeared behind a bluff.

Then I drove on up the lane and stopped again in front of the big iron gates with the white stucco lodge with green Spanish tiles set on one side. Cigales were singing somewhere and the heat was coming up hot and sticky from the earth now. I sighed. It looked like being another pretty swell day. I played Haydn's Trumpet Concerto on the horn button and waited, keeping the motor idled back.

The man-mountain showed in the blackness of the lodge-doorway.

"Mr Larsen's expecting me," I called.

The big man nodded and raised his fist. I switched off the motor and the silence crawled back in. I waited while he got on the phone to the house. By the time I'd finished my cigarette he had reappeared in the doorway. He walked toward the gate as I stubbed out the butt in my ash-tray. He opened one wing of the gate and come on over to the car.

He still wore the faded blue jeans tucked into top-boots. His angry red face didn't look any less angry. Today he wore a faded blue shirt that was stained with sweat. He had the dark cheaters down over his eyes again but I could feel the hard, angry pupils studying me from behind them. I wondered what gave him such a chip on his shoulder. Working for Jack Larsen I guessed.

"It's none of my business, Mr Faraday," he grunted. "But word gets around."

I nodded pleasantly enough. Fingers like pork sausages were clamped over the door-edge now. The big man seemed oblivious of the heat that was searing the panel.

"Word about what?" I said.

"About the reason for you being here,"

he said. "You got time to drop in the lodge?"

"It would be cooler than out here," I said.

He nodded. He went over to the other wing of the gate and latched it back. I drove on through and killed the motor. I got out the car and waited while he re-locked the gate. I followed him to the lodge.

It was a sparsely furnished place with a tiled floor and white-washed stone walls but it was cooler in here than outside. The big man sat down on a high stool which commanded a narrow side window where he could watch the gate.

"My name's Simon," he said. "Not that that's important. I just wanted to give you some advice."

I sat down on the edge of a rough wooden desk and looked at him thoughtfully.

"About what?"

"About the girl," he said.

"You know about the girl?" I said.

He gave a twisted grin.

"Who doesn't?" he told the white-washed walls.

He leaned forward and put up one of his pork-sausage fingers.

"I don't know what he told you, Mr Faraday, but Dale Holden's not his daughter."

"I know that already," I said. "I wasn't the last person in town but pretty nearly."

He grinned crookedly again.

"Jack Larsen's never levelled with anyone in his life," he said.

"He certainly seems to inspire a lot of faith in his employees," I said.

The big man spat. The bright jet of saliva arced expertly through the doorway and disappeared into a flower bed.

"I just thought you'd like to know, Mr Faraday," he said. "It might save some time."

He leaned forward again.

"But here's something you don't know. Larsen's got a long-time lady friend. She's pretty sore about the Holden girl."

"Why are you telling me this?" I said.

The giant shrugged.

"Just trying to steer you in the right direction. The girl's disappeared right? Alys might know something about it. There was no love lost between them."

"For a gateman you don't miss much," I said.

The big man got up from the stool. He gave me another expanse of crooked bridgework.

"It's my job to know what goes on around here," he said. "Larsen pays me extra for such tips."

"You're earning your money today," I said.

The grin faded from the giant's face. He pushed the glasses up on to his forehead.

"He's a creep," he said sharply. "He gets the employees he deserves."

He looked me up and down.

"I was a private eye once. Up in San Francisco. Till I got busted."

"What did you do; welsh on the lollipop concession?" I said.

The giant's face clouded over.

"No call for us to quarrel, Mr Faraday," he said. "Get hold of Alys Vermilyea. She's the one who might help. And a jealous woman often gives a lot away."

"Thanks for the tip," I said. "Where can I find her?"

I expected the big man to put the bite on at this point but he surprised me. This case was getting to be full of surprises. He laid a chunky finger alongside his nose.

"In town," he said. "Astor Apartments."

I nodded.

"I'll remember."

I walked back to the Buick and started her up. I could see the big man standing outside the lodge in the rear mirror. He was still standing there when a bend in the drive cut him off.

9

GREG LAURITZEN was standing at the foot of the steps. It looked like he'd been standing there since the last time I came. I killed the motor and got out the Buick. He came over toward me.

"He's in a strange mood, Mr Faraday. I shouldn't be too flip."

"Sure," I said. "I'll watch it. He might bite me in the leg."

Lauritzen shook his head. He didn't seem to have any sense of humour all the time I knew him. Maybe if I'd been in his position I'd have felt the same. We were walking up the steps now. He took me by the arm.

"He's got a couple of his heavies with him. And they've been drinking."

I looked at him.

"This time of the morning?"

Lauritzen sighed.

"All the time lately. Ever since Dale disappeared."

"Or left," I said.

Lauritzen looked at me sharply. He made a slight inclination of his head.

"Or left," he conceded.

He wore a blue blazer with silver buttons today over a blue open-neck sport shirt. He looked quite snappy. Except for the worried look at the back of the eyes.

"You carry a gun?"

"Not normally," I said. "But on this assignment. I've made an exception."

I looked at him again.

"You think I'll need it."

He nodded.

"It might be an idea, Mr Faraday. This could get rough."

"You talking about Larsen or something else?" I said.

Lauritzen led the way through the French windows into the house.

"Just a hunch," he jerked back over his shoulder.

118

"We'll take this up some other time," I said.

Lauritzen looked at me sombrely.

"Will you wait here?"

"Sure. And I'll see you before I go."

Lauritzen went out the far door and left me standing in the room I'd come through the first time I visited the house. It was a library that still smelt musty and neglected. I guessed the only thing Larsen ever read was the racing form. The library had come with the house.

I looked out at the cool green of the terrace. I wondered how Larsen made his money. I'd heard he was on the board of a number of civil aviation companies. Not that that meant anything. Crooks can get into any kind of businesses nowadays. When I first came out I figured him for an ordinary businessman.

I turned as there came a footfall. Lauritzen was back again. He jerked his head at me. He looked pale under the tan.

"He's in a difficult mood," he whispered. "Just take it easy and be careful."

He led the way along the short corridor and through the den with elks' heads.

"There's two characters there," he whispered. "Both armed. The one called Harry is the dangerous one. He's real mean."

"Thanks for the tip," I said. And meant it.

"I'll look out for him."

Lauritzen passed his tongue across dry lips and tapped at the heavy oak door.

"See you later."

I nodded, opened the door and went on in. The blinds were drawn over the windows, throwing the big room into a sort of striped twilight; otherwise things were the same as before. The long bar, the fruit machines, the tiny figure of Jack Larsen sitting at the bar, his diminutive paw gripped round the stem of a glass that looked bigger than he was. There was the stink of stale cigarette-smoke and booze in the air. It was too early in the day for that sort of atmosphere.

In fact any hour of the day was too early for that in my book. I stood just inside the door, adjusting my eyes to the light. Two big forms moved in the gloom. I was aware of watching eyes.

"Come on in, Mr Faraday," Larsen said.

His voice sounded quite normal. I went on over toward him. Today he wore a blue open-neck shirt, blue matching jeans and open-work sandals. His eyes looked bright and glazed now that I was closer up but otherwise he seemed OK. I wondered why he didn't sit the other side of the bar; he would have looked reasonably normal then. A little on the small side, but of average height. You're getting cruel, Faraday, I told myself.

I knocked it off inside my head. I sat down on a stool near Larsen and looked at him steadily.

"You didn't level with me," I told him.

"Mr Larsen don't have to answer to you," a third voice said. It was a blunt, steely voice that was used to being obeyed. It belonged to a trained pug; all those sort of voices sounded alike.

I'd been hearing them around L.A. for more than a decade now. I sighed and shifted on the stool.

The voice came from one of the two big men at the other side of the room. One, who had a chest like a barrel and was dressed in a check-shirt and tan trousers sat on the back of a divan with his feet on the cushions and stared unwinkingly at me. The one who'd spoken was a tanned looking individual with oiled black hair. He had useful shoulders on him and a white tropical suit. In sunlight it would have been dazzling. Even in here it looked pretty cute. He had a red tie which hung limply against his crisp white shirt; it looked like a smear of blood from where I was sitting. The two men were the ones doing the drinking.

"The chimps doing your talking for you or can you handle your own?" I said.

Larsen smiled at me without expressing humour.

"They got privileges around the house," he said.

"Just keep them off my back," I said. "I came up here to talk to you."

The big man in the white suit was on his feet now. I couldn't see his face in the shadow but a little light spilling in through the blinds glinted on his eyeballs.

"You got a big mouth, Faraday," the man in the white suit said.

"And a big fist to back it," I said.

I looked at Larsen.

"You want me to find Dale Holden or not?"

The little man shrugged.

"Of course. What do you think? That was the deal."

"Let's get to it, then," I said.

White-suit was nearer now. He came across the room with slow, deliberate steps. The bigger man sat immobile on the divan; he raised his glass to his mouth and took slow deliberate gulps.

"Cut the crap," I told Larsen. "My time's valuable. You weren't levelling about Dale Holden."

Larsen's eyes were like dead insects.

"So," he said swilling the liquid around in his glass.

"So I don't give a damn about whether she's your fancy pussy or not," I said. "I've got to have the right information if I'm to earn the fee. Otherwise, no deal."

"You got to show Mr Larsen respect, Faraday," the man in the white suit said.

He was still coming on. I figured he was close enough. I turned on the stool and picked up the full bottle of bourbon that was standing on the bar. White-suit jumped, his hand reaching for his pocket. The bottle caught him between the eyes and he went backward like a rocket, jack-knifing over the divan. Before he'd hit the floor and the broken glass had stopped showering, I had Jack Larsen's jacket open. I took out the cannon from his inside pocket and jammed it up against his nostrils, holding his lapels with my left hand. We must have looked like Edgar Bergen and Charlie McCarthy.

"One more dumb play and I'll blow your head off," I said.

The cannon in the big man's hand wavered slightly. Sweat ran down Jack Larsen's temples. His teeth were chattering as he opened his mouth.

"You'd better do as Mr Faraday says, Joey."

The big man put the pistol away in his hip pocket. He got back up on the divan again. He didn't look at the mess on the floor behind him. There was the stink of spilt liquor heavy on the air now. I took Larsen's pistol away from his head and let go of him.

"You can take the cost of the bottle out of the thousand dollars," I said.

Nobody spoke for a moment. Then Larsen straightened his lapels. He dabbed at his forehead with a handkerchief. He was normal now. He gave a crooked smile.

"There's no need to get tough, Faraday," he said. "I was just testing you out. It was only a joke."

"It was the wrong joke," I said. "And the wrong guy."

I sat back on the stool. I still had hold of the pistol and I kept it pointed toward the big man Larsen called Joey. He got the message all right. There was a moaning noise coming from behind the divan now.

I jerked the muzzle of the pistol.

"You better get him some medication," I said. "He's going to have a headache when he comes around."

Larsen turned his eyes toward Joey.

"Take him out," he ordered. "I can handle this."

We waited while the big man got down behind the divan. He picked up white-suit like he was no more than a bag of sweets. It was only then I remembered Lauritzen's remark. He must have been the one called Harry. We sat in silence until the door closed behind them. Larsen waved his hand toward the bar.

"Help yourself."

I shook my head.

126

"Never touch the stuff during the day. Besides, I've handled enough liquor for one morning."

Larsen permitted himself a thin smile. He didn't seem put out by my rough treatment. He seemed to have nerves that settled down pretty quickly. I opened up the pistol. I emptied out the shells and put them and the weapon itself down on the bar. Larsen sat and watched me with expressionless eyes.

"I want the right story, Mr Larsen," I said. "You haven't been levelling from the beginning. You were keen on Dale Holden, right? There's nothing wrong in that. So she disappeared. Maybe she had good reason."

Larsen nodded his head slowly and portentously.

"I wanted to see how you'd make out, Mr Faraday," he said. "I should have known better."

"You know now," I said. "There was more than a love-affair gone sour in this."

Larsen closed his eyes momentarily.

Then he opened them to put his glass to his lips.

"You're right, Mr Faraday."

"I could smell it a mile off," I told him. "She went off with some property of yours. How much?"

Larsen winced when I mentioned money. Now he leaned forward at the bar and fixed me with a penetrating stare.

"Quite a lot, Mr Faraday. A hundred thousand dollars to be precise."

10

THERE was a long silence. I looked down to my toe-caps. It seemed very quiet in the house now.

"I knew there was something," I said. "But not this big."

I looked up at Larsen.

"That's a lot of change to keep loose in the house."

Larsen's eyes looked shifty.

"I have to have plenty of cash in my business. It was a pay-night, you might say. I didn't find out until after Dale had been gone an hour."

"What is your business?" I said.

Larsen shrugged.

"A little of this. A little of that."

"And some of the other," I said. "With that sort of money rolling around loose Dale Holden could have been the target for all sorts of people. But of course you already figured that?"

Larsen sighed.

"I figured it. She clean disappeared after the gateman passed her out."

"She could be anywhere in the States," I said.

"She's still in L.A.," Larsen said in a dead voice. "Don't ask me how I know. I have a big organization. We checked all the air-line flights, long-distance buses, boats."

"You're forgetting private aircraft," I said.

"We didn't miss a thing," Larsen said.

"And came up with nothing," I said. "All right. I'll buy it for the moment. But it would have been a whole lot easier if you'd told me this the first time I came out here."

"It was my mistake, Mr Faraday," Larsen said. "I admit it frankly."

"At least that's something," I said. "You sure that's all you got to tell me?"

"That's the lot, Mr Faraday."

"Because otherwise you're just wasting your thousand dollars," I said.

"It's my thousand dollars," Larsen said simply.

I shrugged.

"You've got a crazy attitude to this whole thing, Mr Larsen, if you don't mind me saying so."

Larsen turned a dull red.

"I do mind you saying so, Mr Faraday."

He gave me a thin smile.

"But though I carry more financial weight I can't argue with you physically."

He paused.

"For the second time in one morning. Especially as I haven't got my hard men here."

I grinned.

"We both lost our tempers," I said. "Let's forget it."

Larsen took another sip at his glass.

"Since we're taking our hair down," he said. "And since you've reminded me it is my money you're spending, perhaps it wouldn't be too much to ask how you're making out?"

131

"That was the idea of coming here," I said. "But I'm getting a lot of lies and a lot of blind alleys. The list of places you gave me wasn't very helpful."

"It was the only leads I got," Larsen said.

"You'd have done better giving me some real leads," I said.

Larsen blinked. His voice still had the rusty tin quality as he replied but something had gone out of it; what was left had a muted, sorrowful note, like some secret sadness was gnawing at his heart.

"I gave you Dora Farrow," he said simply. "She knows everything worth knowing in that field."

"Sure," I said. "She put me on to a crooked bar-tender at The Crazy Horse called Dexter. He tried to shake me down."

Larsen grinned. It had a genuine quality of humour this time.

"I hope you were able to handle him," he said. "He took me once or twice in my earlier days, before I got pull."

"He tried to roll me, then got a guy built like a ten-ton truck to take me apart. I had to alter Dexter's bridgework but I got my money back."

Larsen rubbed the palms of his hands together with a brittle rustling sound in the oppressive silence of the room.

"My money, Mr Faraday," he corrected me softly.

"It will be my money when I've done the job," I said.

Larsen looked at me shrewdly.

"I knew I chose the right man," he said. "But you came up with something?"

I nodded.

"The guy who bounced me was a character called George Holden. The girl's brother. He was worried about her. He said he'd come out here and couldn't get in the place."

Larsen shook his head. He looked worried.

"A man came once," he said. "As big as a house."

"That's the one," I said.

Larsen folded his small hands round

his glass and looked at me sadly.

"He spoke to me and then to Dale," he said. "I had nothing to hide. He didn't say anything about being the girl's brother when I saw him."

"Would you have been surprised?"

Larsen nodded.

"I never saw two people less alike. Except for height. Dale is a big girl."

"So I understand," I said. "So what's your story?"

"The girl didn't want anything to do with him," Larsen said. "So I closed the gate on him. I understand he came up once or twice after that. He threatened to make trouble. But I'm used to that."

Larsen took another sip at his orange-juice.

"You know where he is now?"

I shook my head.

"But he said he'd keep in touch. He doesn't know where the girl is any more than you do."

Larsen shook his head gloomily.

"You sure the girl never said anything about her brother?" I said.

The rusted tin was back in Larsen's voice.

"I already told you, Mr Faraday. Dale wasn't the one to give confidences."

"Even to you?" I said.

Larsen turned pink. He put the glass down on the bar-top in front of him with a heavy thud.

"Least of all to me."

"I thought you were fond of her," I said.

Larsen showed signs of irritation. Not that I blamed him. I was acting like he was the chief suspect instead of the client.

"I was, Mr Faraday."

He paused.

"Am," he continued. "Let's face it. The girl only came to me because of my money. But I had a genuine feeling for her."

I got up. There didn't seem much point in going on with the interview.

"And when she'd got what she wanted she skipped," I said. "It seems a pretty straightforward story."

Larsen moved convulsively in his position at the bar; his small hands clenched round the stem of his glass.

"Except that I'd like my money back."

"And the girl," I corrected him.

Larsen turned burning eyes on to me.

"And the girl," he said heavily.

"I'll see what I can do," I told him.

I left him sitting at the bar and went on out.

I met Greg Lauritzen in the corridor. He must have been hanging around for news. He grinned when he saw me.

"Say, you certainly worked that punk over," he said enthusiastically. "What did you do to him?"

"A lucky shot," I said. "A bottle of bourbon in the right place."

Lauritzen grinned again. We walked through into the den.

"They just took him off to hospital," he said. "Looks like he'll be out of action for some time."

"You're breaking my heart," I said.

We were back through on to the

terrace by now. Lauritzen looked round carefully though it was obvious there wasn't anyone within two hundred yards of us.

"All the same I'd be careful, Mr Faraday," he said. "That other ape's still around. And he and Harry were pretty close."

"I'll watch my step," I said. "But they won't try anything without Larsen's say-so."

Lauritzen looked at me curiously.

"What really happened in there?"

I told him the basic details. Lauritzen licked his lips and his eyes had a strange glitter.

"You shook Larsen like a rat and got away with it," be said in a dazed voice. "That I'd like to have seen."

I shook my head.

"It didn't do much for my ego," I said. "Using muscle on a midget."

An irritated expression passed across Lauritzen's face.

"You misunderstand me, Mr Faraday. It's what he represents. Men have been found floating in the bay for staring at Larsen in a public restaurant."

"You don't say," I said. "You must remind me to pick my clients more carefully in future." I sat down in a cane chair and looked at the secretary thoughtfully.

"But as long as he is my client we'd better go on with this thing."

Lauritzen nodded. With his blue blazer with the silver buttons he looked like a yachtsman on his day off.

"There's a woman called Alys Vermilyea," he said.

"I wondered when you'd get to her," I said.

Lauritzen looked surprised.

"So you know about her already."

"I heard a vague rumour," I said.

Lauritzen's eyes raked my face. He had a look of grudging admiration in them.

"You don't miss much, Mr Faraday."

"I try not to," I said. "But I've missed a hell of a lot on this case. Everybody seems to be telling lies."

Lauritzen gave a wry smile.

"Not everybody, Mr Faraday. You're welcome to check my statement."

"There may be exceptions," I said. "What about Alys Vermilyea?"

Lauritzen got up and put his hands in his blazer pockets; he looked like an old ad out of *The Yachtsman* as he stood there.

"She used to be the favourite until Dale came along. I hear she's pretty sore."

I sat and looked at him without saying anything. I decided I wouldn't say anything about my conversation with the gateman. He could be a useful source and I might need him in future. The set-up at Larsen's place seemed like something out of Hitler's establishment at The Wolf's Lair; with everyone spying on everyone else. But none of this was getting me any closer to the elusive Dale Holden. I sighed. Lauritzen looked at me sympathetically.

"I know how you feel, Mr Faraday."

"Nobody does," I said. "What did

you say the Vermilyea woman's address was?"

"I didn't, Mr Faraday. It's 2222 Astor Apartments. But don't tell her I sent you."

I nodded. I went back down the steps and left him standing there. I had a lot to think about as I drove back in to town.

11

THE Astor Apartments was a fairly chintzy lay-out set in an acre or so of carefully tended gardens. I slotted the Buick into a parking area with a white board marked: PRIVATE: RESIDENTS ONLY and killed the motor. I got out and went up the broad marble steps; there was a cocktail bar with a blue neon sign blazing in the bright sunlight on one side and candy-striped awnings running all the way across the entrance.

In the foyer there were chocolate brown carpets, a lot of walnut fittings, well-oiled rubber-plants in teak trunking, and imitation marble walls. I went over to the board on the right-hand side of the foyer and studied the lay-out; Apartment 2222 was on the third floor. I glanced around the lobby. Apart from two middle-aged men deep in conversation on one of the divans; the girl at the reception desk; and the commissionaire standing just inside the swing-doors, the place seemed empty.

I got in the elevator-cage and buttoned my way up to the third floor. Two old ladies got in as I quitted the teak box; they had two Dalmatians on leashes and they looked like someone was burning old linoleum under their nostrils. It was that kind of joint. I sighed and went along the blue-carpeted corridor where dim lights burned. I went to the left first but found I'd got the wrong direction.

I came back and went on down, looking at the phosphor bronze numerals screwed to the wall at the side of the doors; 2222 was the last apartment on the right at the far end. I thumbed the button and heard the faint metallic buzzing away in the interior.

Nothing happened so I leaned on the button again; perhaps Miss Vermilyea was out. It would be about par for the case. I sighed again.

I waited another minute and then gave

the button a final burst. A Judas-hole in the door opened and a watery eye surveyed me.

"I'm not deaf. What the hell do you want?" a blurred voice said.

I couldn't tell whether it was a woman or a man.

"I'm looking for a Miss Vermilyea," I said. "Would you be she?"

The eye blinked rapidly.

"You swallowed a dictionary or something? Sure I'm her."

I grinned.

"Miss Alys Vermilyea?"

"How many they got around L.A.?" the voice said.

"You made your point, Miss Vermilyea," I said. "I'd like a word with you."

"Shoot ahead," the Vermilyea woman said.

I made my voice sound as smooth as possible.

"We can't talk out here. What I've got to say is private."

The eye swivelled for a long moment as its owner took me in.

143

"Who are you?"

"My name's Faraday," I said. "I'm a private investigator. It's important."

"A dick, eh?" the woman said. "Just my luck. You got any identification?"

I reached in my breast-pocket for the photostat of my licence in the leather holder and held it up for her to look at. She was apparently satisfied because the trap slammed shut. There was the rattle of a bolt and chain. The door opened on the chain. A blonde woman was standing in the narrow opening; she regarded me silently for a moment longer.

"You spell trouble to me, Mr Faraday," the Vermilyea number said. "I suppose you'd better come in. But I haven't got all day."

"My time's important too," I said.

The woman nodded. She unlatched the door and held it open for me to pass through. She slammed and locked it behind me.

"Is it about Jack Larsen?"

I nodded.

144

"In some ways."

An anxious expression passed across the blonde's face.

"He send you?"

I shook my head.

"He doesn't know I'm here."

The blonde let out a sigh of relief.

"That's something anyway."

She looked at me curiously.

"You look like you could use a drink."

I shook my head.

"I wouldn't mind something long and cool. But not too much alcohol this time of day."

Alys Vermilyea had a shrewd expression on her face.

"I thought you private eyes spent all the time drinking."

I grinned.

"Only in the movies."

The blonde shrugged.

"I'm learning something every day."

She ushered me across the small hall into a crowded living room; it was pretty luxuriously appointed but she had too much crammed into it. There were a lot of china ornaments along the mantelpiece and others in glass cases scattered about the room; I went over and looked at one or two. They were all figures of various breeds of dog. The Vermilyea number looked at me enthusiastically.

"Great, aren't they? I got one of the best collections on the Coast."

"I wouldn't know," I said. "I'm no connoisseur. But you've sure sure got a lot of them."

The woman smiled again, like I'd paid her a compliment.

"One drink coming up," she said. "Make yourself comfortable."

She went over to a buffet made of bleached maple and started fiddling about with ice and long glasses. The sun spilled in through the Venetian blinds and made stippled shadows on the parquet. She came back and put the long, cold glass in my hand. She went back and fetched her own.

Alys Vermilyea was a handsome woman of about thirty-eight. She had a good figure and everything else to go with it. Her blonde hair looked natural but she obviously had it fixed every other day. She had a high, broad forehead; a tanned complexion with tiny lines that were beginning to show at the corners of the eyes and mouth.

The eyes were a faded blue; the mouth was wide and sensuous; the teeth white and well-kept. She had a strong, determined chin and an expression that denoted both force of character and good humour. Even allowing for Larsen's way of life and the girl's photograph I thought he'd be a fool to throw her over.

Right now she had a strained look around the mouth and an empty, tired expression in the eyes that added up to too little sleep at night and too many highballs during the day. I noticed she was having the same drink as myself; that is, about ninety per cent lime-juice, five per cent ice and the rest alcohol. It was the right sort of drink for the morning.

The Vermilyea number sat down on a black leather divan across from me and looked over her glass. Though it was past midday she wore a black chiffon housecoat of the type I thought had gone out with Bogart movies; not that they've really gone out. They're back again on TV if they've ever been away, but I didn't think people still wore that sort of stuff in real life.

Not that I was complaining; she looked all right in it. I could see what she was wearing underneath. It wasn't much. She was showing a lot of leg the way she was sitting; she had good legs too and they were evenly tanned. They ended up in black mules with gold clocks on them. She wasn't putting me on, though; you can always tell. The outfit wasn't for effect; she sat quite unselfconsciously and waited for me to tell her why I was there.

I didn't keep her waiting long.

"I'm looking for a girl called Dale Holden," I said.

Alys Vermilyea sighed. She put down her glass on an ebony table with a thump.

"That bitch," she said evenly. "It figures."

She fumbled around for a cigarette. I got my pack out.

"Have one of mine."

She took it and I lit up for her.

"Thanks."

She leaned back on the divan and feathered smoke at the ceiling.

"What makes you think I'd know where she was? Or be interested in finding her, come to that?"

"I don't blame you for your attitude," I said. "I heard Larsen gave you the air for the Holden number."

Alys Vermilyea looked at me evenly and took another nervous drag at the cigarette.

"Who told you that?"

I shrugged.

"It's my job to find out things."

"It's not a very nice job, Mr Faraday."

She bit the words off short, giving them a sharp snap. I nodded.

"I'm inclined to agree with you, Miss Vermilyea. For what it's worth I think

149

Jack Larsen was crazy to do what he did, but I'm not here to sit in judgment on my clients."

The Vermilyea woman blew out more smoke and looked at me thoughtfully.

"Thanks for the kind word, anyway. You look as though you might be human, Mr Faraday."

"I try," I said. "I thought we might do business together."

Her eyes narrowed.

"In what way?"

"An exchange of information."

She folded one shapely knee over the other and sat frowning at the gold clock on her right mule.

"It could be," she said. "What had you in mind?"

"We help one another," I said.

The Vermilyea number frowned again.

"Sounds all right. I thought you were working for Jack Larsen."

"So I am," I said. "But I'm interested in the truth more than anything."

The blonde woman gave me a dry look.

"It makes a change," she told the wall-paper.

"You said Dale Holden was a bitch," I said. "What exactly did you mean?"

Alys Vermilyea's eyes were clouded and angry as she looked down into her glass.

"Exactly what I said, Mr Faraday. A bitch, pure and simple. She was taking Jack for everything she could get. It was as plain as that, only he couldn't see it."

"Did you tell him that?"

The Vermilyea number gave a short laugh.

"You don't know Jack Larsen very well, mister. He's a tiny man, sure. But he's got people round him. You wouldn't understand . . ."

"Maybe I would," I said. "I laid one of them out today."

The blonde woman stopped suddenly with her glass half way to her mouth; she looked at me silently for a moment.

"Which one?"

"A character in a white suit, called Harry," I said.

151

There was a strange expression on the Vermilyea number's face; it was a smile of great charm and simplicity. She swivelled round on the divan to face me.

"You don't say, Mr Faraday. First time I ever heard of anything like that. What happened to him?"

"He got out of line," I said. "I caught him with a full bottle of bourbon. He went off to hospital."

Alys Vermilyea chuckled; she went on gurgling to herself for a couple of minutes or so.

"Now I know there is a God," she said.

Before I could stop her she swivelled and dropped part of her housecoat; I could see white scars across the area of her shoulder-blades. She shrugged the housecoat back into position angrily.

"You know what did that, Mr Faraday?"

"They look like cigarette burns."

The blonde woman nodded sombrely.

"Harry did that. On Jack's instructions. Just because I kicked up when the

Holden woman started muscling in."

"Why the hell do you bother with him?" I said.

Alys Vermilyea took a long pull at her drink.

"Someone like you would never understand, Mr Faraday. But I got it real bad for Jack Larsen. So why would I be telling you where Dale Holden could be found? So you could bring her back to Jack?"

I shook my head.

"She ran off with some money," I said. "She might be dead for all I know."

The blonde wrinkled up her eyes until they were mere pin-points.

"I hadn't thought of that. You think there's a chance?"

"I don't honestly know, Miss Vermilyea," I said. "But I've been hired to find her. So far everyone on the case has been telling lies, including Jack Larsen. It doesn't help any."

The Vermilyea woman started laughing again.

"It figures," she said.

She put down her glass on the table and sat in thought for a moment, her hands locked round her kneecap.

"You tried George?" she said. "He was looking for her."

"You mean George Holden?" I said. "Her brother?"

The Vermilyea woman stared at me; I knew what she was going to say before she opened her mouth.

"Brother, hell! I'm talking about George Marcos. Dale was his woman before she came to L.A. George was pretty sore. He went up to see Jack and got thrown off."

"Great," I said. "That makes a hundred per cent lie average. That's pretty good even for me."

"You're too pure for L.A., Mr Faraday," Alys Vermilyea said. "You're mixing in a world full of creeps and chisellers."

"Only in Jack Larsen's world," I said. "There are other worlds."

Alys Vermilyea looked at me sadly. "I never moved in them," she said.

"How come you know so much about

George Marcos?" I said.

The blonde woman shrugged.

"Simple. He came here to see me. He had the same questions you're asking now. I gave him the same answers. He didn't like it very much."

I finished off my drink and put it down. I had a lot to think about.

"How did he know where to find you?" I said.

Alys Vermilyea got up to mix herself another drink.

"It wouldn't be difficult," she said. "It's a well-known story, Jack and me. Besides, there's a bar-keep over at The Crazy Horse who makes a living by peddling such information."

"We've met," I said. "I had to lean on him too."

Delight showed in the Vermilyea number's face as she turned around.

"This is my day, Mr Faraday," she said, coming over and throwing her arms around my neck.

"I guess I found a friend."

12

I GOT outside some lunch at a dinette and found a pay-booth. Alys Vermilyea had been very helpful. She'd asked me to stay on to have a meal with her but I had other things to do. Any other time I might have been interested but I had to get results soon; I'd been going round in circles so far. The Holden girl might just as well not exist for all the good I was doing.

Come to that I didn't know what good it would do seeing George Holden; or Marcos if Alys Vermilyea was right. I shrugged gloomily. I knew damn well Alys Vermilyea was right. There was something about her; she may have been on the make but she was honest so far as that went. And she had too much class for people like Larsen.

I'd told her I'd keep an eye open and report on the state of things in Larsen's camp; in return and for starters she'd given me Marcos' present address. That was something at any rate. And it might lead to better things. I'd kept my eye on the rear-mirror all the way across town; I had in mind Larsen's gorillas.

White-suit was out of action all right but the other soldier would still be around; after what had happened I figured Larsen might put a tail on me in case I found the Holden girl. She must be the most elusive character in L.A. history. There had to be a loose end somewhere, but I couldn't find it.

I rang Stella. She answered as soon as the dialling tone sounded; I pushed the buton and kept an eye on the street entrance of the dinette. I told her about Holden.

"I'm just going over to a place called the DeLaVigne Apartments," I said. "It's off Court Street."

I waited while she made a note.

"What's the interest there?" Stella said.

"George Holden," I said. "Larsen's ex-girl friend came up with some information. Holden isn't the girl's brother. And his name's not Holden. It's Marcos."

Stella made a deprecatory clicking noise in my ear.

"You're well above par so far, Mike," she said.

"You can say that again," I told her. "Dale was his girlfriend. And he got pretty sore when she shacked up with Larsen."

"It figures," Stella said.

I could see the expression on her face as she bent over her notepad; don't ask me how. It was something to do with the inflexion of her voice.

"We seem to be getting a pretty high percentage of liars on this one, Mike."

"You took the words right out of my mouth," I said.

I lit a cigarette, holding the phone under my chin, keeping my eye on the door of the dinette.

"You might see what you can dig up on a girl called Alys Vermilyea. Larsen

158

was apparently sweet on her before the Holden girl moved in."

Stella took another note.

"She's attractive, of course?"

"Of course," I said.

Stella chuckled.

"What's the set-up there?"

"We've agreed to co-operate," I said. "She wants to get back with Larsen. Don't ask me why. She seems to have money of her own."

"Perhaps it came from Larsen originally," Stella said.

"It's a point," I said.

There was another short silence.

"Anyway, she's already helped on Marcos' address," I said. "We'll just play it by ear."

I put my cigarette down on the shelf in the booth and removed a flake of tobacco from my lip.

"There's something I forgot to tell you, honey. When the Holden girl disappeared a hundred thousand dollars of Larsen's money went with her."

Stella didn't exactly whistle but I could

almost see her lips pucker.

"Noted," she said drily. "No doubt the implications haven't escaped you?"

I grinned.

"Not exactly."

"You back in this afternoon?" Stella said.

"I'll try and make it," I said. "But it won't be until after five."

I rang off and stood finishing my cigarette and frowning at the graffiti scribbled on the wall above the booth mirror. Then I went out, got in the Buick and started making time across town.

I found Court Street all right but I had some difficulty over the DeLaVigne Apartments. I found an empty space by the kerb in the end and slotted the Buick in behind a tourist bus that was full of rubber-necking old ladies with blue-rinsed hair. I saw the fire-plug too late but waited while the bus pulled out before rolling forward into the vacant space. I killed the motor and set fire to a cigarette.

The sun was past its peak but it still had a sting to it. I went down the block a ways and noticed a flight of steps cutting up a strip of hillside which had been sown with grass and carved into flower beds. They were a riot of red and blue at this time of the year. I got to the top of the flight and saw there was a paved piazza.

There were several blocks of white apartment buildings, dazzling in the sun. I saw then I should have pulled off the road about half a mile back and come up the spur which debouched into the parking areas. It didn't matter really and the exercise was doing me good.

The third block was the DeLaVigne Apartments according to the gold anodised lettering screwed over the entrance canopy. There was a fountain playing in the middle of the plaza; a kiosk selling cigarettes and magazines; a restaurant; and a big board that gave all the names of tenants on printed cards.

They had a typed alphabetical run-down in a glassed-in case under the main board and I ran my eye down that. The name Marcos was there all right. He was using his real name and had given the Vermilyea woman his real address; that was something. It was ruining my view of human nature; someone had spoken the truth for once. I grinned and went on over the ground-floor plaza.

Apartment 44 was on the first floor so I walked up the teak staircase at the side of the lobby. It was about halfway down the first corridor on the right. I pressed the button and waited for my man to show. I heard the faint sound of the buzzer in the distance and waited again, keeping my thumb on it. It was the story of my life. Nothing moved in the corridor and there was no sound, except the faint hum of the air-conditioning.

I took my finger off the button and stared at the points of my shoes; that made a refreshing change. They were scuffed like usual. I sighed and hit the button again. Nothing happened. It looked like my man wasn't home. That figured too. I tried the door. It was locked like it would be. I went on down the corridor. At the end there was plate-glass, with a door set in it.

The door led to a wide balcony which ran all the way round the building. There were cane chairs set about and all the other apparatus of idle living. The door was standing ajar, with a bunch of keys in the lock. I looked at the keys and then decided against borrowing them. One of the maids might come for the keys and then there would only be trouble. Whereas strolling along a balcony gained by an open door was only idle curiosity and not an indictable offence.

I went on through the door on to the balcony. The apartments were divided by white trunking with flowering plants but they were only a formality; they didn't stretch all the way across and there was a broad passage at the balcony front. I walked on down it; there were a few people sitting out taking the sun but they didn't even glance at me.

I walked on, looking like I lived there; I'd made a mental note of where 44 ought to be but I needn't have bothered. The numbers of the Apartments were painted in black figures at the end of each section of trunking; they were evens on this side. I ignored the mute appeal of a blonde in a two-piece swim-suit wearing dark cheaters and with all the equipment to go with the costume. I hadn't got the time this afternoon. Besides, it was too hot.

The blonde lay on a horizon-blue beach bed and twisted her legs about in a provocative manner. Then she lifted herself on one elbow and stared at me over the glasses. I pretended to ignore her and almost ran into the end of the next section of trunking. Her thin tinkle of laughter followed me all the way down the balcony.

Apartment 44 was identical to the others; white walls, Spanish metal grilles at the windows, striped sun-blinds over the tops of the doors and the porticos. I lit another cigarette and looked around. No-one else was in sight and no-one was taking any notice of me. The balcony door was double-framed with glass in each section. It was unlocked. I put my spent match-stalk back in the box and put that in my pocket.

I opened up the door and stepped through. The Venetian blinds at the windows on this side were drawn and it was dim and cool in the interior. The room was a big one, with a stone fireplace up at one end for effect. There was a red Swedish telephone lying on the carpet halfway between a glass-topped table on which it obviously normally stood and a leather armchair.

I went over and stood frowning down at it, adjusting my eyes to the light. Unless Marcos did all his phoning on the floor like a teenager something was wrong here. If the phone had fallen, or been knocked over, it hadn't dislodged the receiver; that was still in position. I didn't touch it.

I went around the room. I didn't know what I was looking for but I'd know it when I saw it. There was nothing in the room of any interest. It had that dead, impersonal look that rented apartments often have. Marcos must have had some money to afford this place. I opened up the far door, using my handkerchief on the bronze knob. It led to a long, narrow hallway.

The first door led into a small kitchen, overlooking the blank wall of the apartment block opposite. There were some cups and stuff on the steel draining board that held coffee-grounds and the remains of food. It looked like somebody's breakfast. The tap dripped suddenly in the silence. It got on my nerves after a bit so I crossed over and turned it off, still using the handkerchief. I didn't know why. It was just a hunch. But my hunches often work out.

There was nothing in the kitchen so I didn't stay long. There was another small room with lounging chairs and a TV set. That was a little more interesting. It had a jacket hanging over the back of a chair. I went through the pockets. There was nothing personal in there.

There was a small toilet just down the

corridor. That was empty like I figured. That left just two more doors. The bedroom was a big room, overlooking the balcony. The blinds at the windows were drawn. The bed had been made and everything looked normal. There was a long wardrobe of white wood one side of the room, with sliding doors.

I opened it up; there were three or four suits, shabby but carefully brushed and pressed, hanging on the pegs. They were about Marcos' size. I spent a few minutes going through the pockets. Like I figured it was a waste of time. There was nothing of any interest in any of the pockets, except a box of matches, a dirty handkerchief and a half-eaten bag of peanuts. I put everything back as I'd found it and closed the door, still using my handkerchief.

I crossed over to the head of the bed. There was a low table of carved walnut next the bed, bearing a lamp with an earthenware standard and an ash-tray with a monogram and the legend of the DeLaVigne Apartments on it. The third object on the table was what interested me. It was a big silver photo-frame. Unlike most things of its kind it was lying face-downward on the surface of the table. I turned it over, taking care not to leave any finger-prints. The frame was empty. Someone had removed the picture it had once contained.

I stood looking down at it and then put it back as I'd found it. Interesting. Perhaps it had held a picture of Dale Holden and Marcos; maybe Dale Holden alone. Who knows? It might have been important. Or not. It was just something else to bear in mind. I sighed and finished off my cigarette. I went over and opened the window wider to let the smoke out.

Then I crushed out the butt and put it back in the package. I waited until the atmosphere was clear and then put the window strut back as I'd found it. That left the last door. I almost didn't bother. But I'm nothing if not thorough. So I went through the motions.

The last door led to the bathroom. It

wasn't locked either. The place was full of steam. When it cleared sufficiently I could see the bath was full. George Holden or Marcos or whatever his real name was was sitting in the bath. He was quite naked and quite dead. Someone had shot him at point-blank range as he was having his bath. It was heavy stuff which had left a big hole above the ribs. His white curly hair looked like it had been dusted with frost.

Blood had trickled down from the mouth and ears and nose to join the rest. The bath was full of blood too. Marat wasn't in it. I stood there for a few seconds more, with a lot of blank thoughts chasing themselves round inside my skull. A nerve in my cheek twitched somewhere.

Marcos' clothes were on a chair by the edge of the bath. I could tell by the way they'd been run through and then replaced that a pro had been at work. I didn't bother to search. It would have been a waste of time. I went away quickly and quietly, let myself out the main door of the apartment, using the handkerchief again, and went back to the car as fast as possible without attracting attention. I started breathing again as soon as the Buick had taken me three blocks away.

13

"NOT exactly your best case, Mike."

"There's some logic in your reasoning, honey," I said. "It's been a rough day."

Stella smiled sympathetically. It was nearly dusk and the neon outside the window was spreading red, yellow and green fingers across the furniture and fittings. Stella sat on the edge of her desk and swung a shapely leg. It made me nervous so I got up and went over to the window. I closed the blinds and came on back.

"Time to shut up shop," I said.

"Except for the coffee," Stella said. "It won't be long."

"I'd forgotten," I said.

Stella gave me a sharp look.

"You must be ill, Mike," she said. "It's the first time."

"I've got a lot on what's left of my mind," I said.

I went over to sit back at the desk again. I looked at Stella moodily. Today she wore a thin brown sweater with a polo neck. It couldn't have been wool; maybe it was silk. I was never very hot on the materials women wore.

It had a small gold brooch pinned to the right breast; it flashed and glinted every time Stella changed position. Her pencil-slim blue skirt was riding way up. She looked as neat and shiny as a button, like always. The lamps glittered on the bright gold of her hair. The blue eyes were lost in shadow as she stared at me thoughtfully. She shifted again then and the brooch made a little yellow flame in the shadows of the office.

"How that glittering taketh me," I said.

Stella smiled again, revealing even white teeth.

"You quoted that before," she said.

"And no doubt I'll be quoting it again one of these days," I said.

Stella slid off the desk with a lithe movement and went over to the alcove. I heard the snick as she switched the percolator off. I sat back, savouring the aroma of fresh coffee. This was one hell of a case and I didn't know where to go from here on in.

"Let's go over the facts, Mike," Stella said, coming back. She sat down on the edge of the desk again.

"What facts?" I said.

Stella tapped with a gold pencil on even teeth. Then she got up again. I heard her cross the waiting room and then the click as she locked the outer door. The light in the waiting room went out. I sat on blankly while she fetched the cups. She put a full one down on my blotter together with a tin of biscuits.

"Sugar coming up."

I sat back and inhaled the aroma and wondered when I'd see some light; the image of Dale Holden floated to the surface of my cup. It was a composite of the two photographs I'd seen. One a

173

blurred blow-up of a half-nude showgirl, the other a more subdued studio study.

Stella was back again now. She left the sugar bowl on my blotter, put her own cup down on the corner of my desk and went back to sit on the edge of her own. Her eyes searched my face.

"Let's just run over what we know about the set-up, Mike."

"That shouldn't take more than three seconds," I said.

Stella smiled. It seemed to light up the office.

"I thought nothing fazed Faraday Investigations?" she said.

I shrugged.

"Everyone hits rock bottom sometimes, even me."

I opened my eyes and grinned at her. I sat up and started drinking the coffee.

"That's my boy," Stella said.

She came over and her lips lightly brushed my cheek. I felt the echo of it all the way down to my fallen arches. Stella was back on her perch before I could make a move. She went on like nothing had happened.

I put the sugar in my cup and tasted the coffee. It was just right, like always. Stella drank hers in silence for a moment, watching me intently. The distant noise of traffic went on like a giant insect beyond the window blinds.

"Jack Larsen calls you in because his daughter's missing," Stella said. "Larsen is probably a millionaire, almost certainly a crook."

"Check on all points," I said.

I rooted out a Florida Delight from the mass of biscuits in the tin and dunked it in my coffee. Stella made a little moue. I went on dunking anyway.

"Only Dale Holden wasn't his daughter but his girl-friend," she said. "The secretary, Lauritzen, has his own axe to grind. We still don't know where he stands."

"In it up to his neck," I said. "He was sweet on the girl too, remember. But I don't think he'd have a good motive. If he'd had his way he'd have disappeared with the girl and the money."

"You think he knows about the money, Mike?"

I shrugged.

"He didn't act like he did. But it's possible. Even if he did he might not tell me for a number of reasons."

"Like he'd have it stashed away somewhere," Stella said.

"This gets better and better," I told her.

She grinned and put down her cup. She leaned back on the desk and went on.

"He is the secretary, Mike. Surely Larsen would have told him about the money."

"Maybe not," I said. "They don't get on very well. There's another thing too. The hundred thousand was almost certainly hot money. So Larsen wouldn't want the police in."

"Which was why he employed you?"

"Check," I said. "So if he wouldn't tell the police he probably wouldn't tell Lauritzen. He only told me as an afterthought. All he wanted was the girl on the face of it."

Stella went on, "You scratch around and come up with a crooked barkeep who puts Holden on to you."

"Marcos," I corrected her. "The girl's brother, only he isn't her brother but another boy friend. Are you following this all right?"

Stella grinned happily.

"I'm supposed to be telling you, remember? I keep the records around here."

I picked up my coffee cup again and finished it off. Stella went back to the alcove to re-fill it for me. I felt my brain was bursting with the pressure of non-facts. Stella put the re-filled cup back.

"That brings us to Alys Vermilyea," she went on. "Larsen's ex, who was deposed to make way for the Holden girl. Marcos came to see her and she wasn't able to help."

"Maybe she had the whole thing fixed up," I said. "Had the girl put away or helped her to blow town."

Stella shook her head.

"You don't know much about female psychology, Mike. In the first place no woman is going to help her rival to a hundred thousand free smackers. And additionally, if Larsen found out she was behind Dale Holden skipping it wouldn't have helped her with him at all."

"You're probably right," I said gloomily.

"So all we got to do now is to find Dale Holden," Stella said. "Plus the character who killed George Marcos."

"Sure," I said. "I didn't realize the case was so simple."

Stella's smile was dazzling by this time.

"What about Larsen's heavies," she said. "You're forgetting them. The one you downed will probably be out for a week or two. What about the gorilla?"

I stared at her for a long moment.

"It's an angle, honey," I said slowly. "He is a member of the household. Someone must know why Dale Holden skipped and how."

"And if she's still alive," Stella said.

178

"Larsen checked the airports, bus stations and hotels," I said. "A character like him would be pretty thorough."

"She couldn't just disappear," Stella said.

I leaned back in my chair and stared at the bland surface of my coffee.

"She's giving a damned good imitation of it," I said.

"Don't forget the Smith-Wesson," Stella said.

I tapped my chest.

"I'm wearing it. But thanks, anyway."

"Just part of the service," Stella said.

I sat back frowning. Stella got off the desk and put down her cup.

"Something wrong?"

"Maybe," I said. "I don't know yet. I just remembered something."

Stella stood there, her head on one side, the empty cup in her hand, looking at me.

"Like what?"

"I gave Marcos a card with my business address on," I said. "I just hope it hasn't fallen into the wrong hands."

Stella wrinkled up her nose.

"I don't follow you, Mike."

"I went through Marcos' stuff in his apartment fairly closely," I said. "I didn't give the card a thought then, it's true. But it certainly wasn't there."

Stella put the cup down and stood in thought for a moment.

"What about the stuff in the bathroom?"

I shook my head.

"I didn't check but a pro had been through it. The pockets were turned over. Whoever killed Marcos wouldn't have overlooked it."

"Unless Marcos destroyed it or threw it away," Stella said.

"What reason would he have?" I said. "He wanted to contact me again."

"Just a thought," Stella said. "Why are you so worried, anyway?"

"Someone might try to frame me," I said.

I got up and switched off the desk light.

"Or maybe shake me down."

Stella went over to the alcove and

started rinsing cups. She put her head round the ground-glass screen.

"What for?"

"Just a hunch," I said. "Supposing someone else turned up after Marcos was hit. They might think I'd gone off with the hundred thousand."

"But Marcos didn't have it," Stella said.

I shrugged.

"Who knows? The guy who shot him, perhaps. But nobody else. Maybe someone might think I'd cooled Marcos and taken the money. Which puts me in a spot."

"You're always in a spot," Stella said affectionately. "You've got too much imagination."

She finished in the alcove and came over toward the desk again.

"Maybe the police found it?"

"They'd have been here long before now," I said. "Besides, the apartment was empty. It would have been swarming with blue if the law had been called in."

Stella let her breath out in a long, low sound.

"Well, take care, Mike."

I tapped my pocket.

"I've got some fire-power now," I said.

14

I WALKED back a couple of blocks to fetch the Buick from my usual garage. There was hardly anybody about on the sidewalk. Stella had already gone. I'd stayed on a bit to pound my brains a while longer. It didn't do any good and I'd given it up. I called in at a drug-store to buy a pack of cigarettes and lit one up. It was a hot, lowering night which smelt of rain. I felt we'd get it before the evening was over.

I walked on down through the alley which led to the garage, the Smith-Wesson making a nice pressure against my chest all the way. The negro in the scarlet shirt who always sat in the all-night glass booth gave me a smile which seemed to break his face in half. He was always cheerful and ever since I could remember he always wore a scarlet shirt on night duty. He was reading a comic book and something seemed to have taken him because I could hear his chuckles clear down the ramp.

It was dark in here, with only the occasional naked bulb burning in a wall socket, but I knew the way and picked a route between the concrete piers to the area where the Buick was stashed. My footsteps made melancholy echoes under the cement roof and a tap was dripping on to the bare floor somewhere. I went over to where it was; I turned it off and slid the fire-bucket underneath it.

I stubbed out my cigarette on the wall by my shoulder and flipped it into the bucket. There were only a few cars in here and the Buick was up the far end. I walked on down, turning over the problems of Dale Holden in my mind. They seemed insoluble. I rounded the shimmering mass of a scarlet Cadillac and made for the Buick.

Something stuck in my mind that Stella had said; something to do with the business card I'd given Holden. I still called him that though I'd no doubt

Alys Vermilyea had told me the truth and that his real name was Marcos. It was ironic that about the only person on the case who had levelled was the former mistress of Larsen. Everyone else was lying to their teeth.

It wasn't only that the Vermilyea woman had given me the right address; there was something about her whole attitude that sat right. And anyway, women who'd been thrown over were usually too angry and bitter to do anything but make with the right facts. She was different; she was bitter all right, but she was calm too, like she'd thought everything out.

I stopped by the rear of the scarlet Cadillac; I wondered whether Alys Vermilyea had known that I'd find the Marcos character dead? In which case it might mean that Larsen had something to do with it. Though I couldn't really see what motive he had. He'd already thrown Marcos off his property. But jealousy of Dale Holden could have been in back of it. I was getting to like the girl's character less and less the more I discovered about her.

I grinned to myself in the semi-darkness of the garage; I hadn't found out anything if it came down to it. Everyone involved seemed to see a different woman; Larsen a glittering mistress; Lauritzen a sophisticated but basically decent girl; Marcos a lost love. I didn't know exactly how Alys Vermilyea saw her except that it was obviously from a different angle.

I had a hunch then; I thought I'd give the Vermilyea woman a ring. I had to see her again some time. There was a public phone on the wall up the other end of the garage. I turned round and went back over to it. There was a light on the wall over the phone and I fumbled for the switch.

There was a directory in the glass wall-cupboard where the phone was and I looked up the number. I put the book back on the shelf and dialled. I stood listening to the dialling tone and tasting the stale tobacco in my mouth.

There was no reply. I hung in there for a couple of minutes but she was obviously out. I gave a heavy sigh. I put the phone back on the rest, shut the door of the booth and turned out the light.

I walked back over to the Buick, my size nines making melancholy echoes under the concrete roof. I opened up the driving door. A heavy form stirred on the passenger seat. The big man had deep-ringed eyes and a hard, durable look. I'd seen him before. More importantly he had a Magnum trained rock-steady on my navel. Its muzzle looked as big as a railroad tunnel.

"Just get in, Faraday," he said in a voice like rusted metal. "No tricks or I splatter your guts all over the wall."

I got in the driving seat very slowly and closed the door of the Buick behind me. I looked at the big man steadily.

"I wouldn't want that to happen," I told him.

He opened his lips about two millimetres.

"Just button your mouth and unbutton your jacket."

I did like he said. He reached over and slid out the Smith-Wesson. His smile opened up another millimetre. There was no humour in it. He broke the gun with his disengaged hand and spilled out the shells on the floor of the car. Then he did a curious thing; for him, I mean. He put the gun back in my holster.

"That's better," he said. "Drive."

I started up the motor.

"Anywhere special?"

"I'll tell you where to turn."

I tooled the car out down the ramp and on to the street. He nodded and I slotted in to the traffic, turning left. We drove across town for a few minutes.

"How's your friend?" I said.

He shrugged.

"Harry? He'll live. That was a piece of luck."

I shook my head.

"That wasn't luck. I'm one of the best

bottle-throwers in the business."

He grunted but didn't make any reply: the Magnum was still trained steadily on my gut. It would have blown my insides out if he'd pulled the trigger. So I didn't try anything. Not that I would have while I was driving. The big man had been watching the passing traffic and the intersections, but I could see by his expression that he wasn't missing a move.

"Jack Larsen know you're here?" I said.

He shook his head.

"Jack Larsen doesn't pay me for the evenings," he said. "My time's my own then."

"That's an original thought," I said. "Does this mean you're in business for yourself?"

"What do you think, shamus?"

"I think Jack Larsen's surrounded himself with some pretty unreliable people," I said.

I took my eyes off the road for a fraction and looked him in the eyes.

What I saw there wasn't very reassuring.

"You didn't chill Marcos by any chance?"

The big man's expression didn't change but his eyes narrowed momentarily.

"So you were there," I said.

He nodded.

"I was there. What did you do with the money?"

I sighed.

"I didn't kill him if that's what you mean. And I thought the money was supposed to be a secret."

He shook his head.

"That little girl had a flapping mouth."

"Had?" I said.

He gave me a frozen look.

"Don't get fancy with me, Faraday. You were at Marcos' place. In my book you killed him. Which means you got the money. Looks like I got to shake it out of you."

"You used the past tense for the Holden girl," I said.

"What's that supposed to mean?"

I turned right at his nodded direction.

190

I waited for a red signal to change to green.

"It could mean the girl's dead," I said.

He shook his head.

"I don't know anything about that. It was my job and Harry's to guard her."

"You did a lousy job," I said.

The big man's eyes smouldered; for a moment he looked genuinely hurt. Evidently I'd struck at his professional pride.

"She could be anywhere," he said. "She skipped. Didn't Larsen tell you? Harry and me checked everywhere."

"Where were you when she skipped?" I said.

The big man sighed. The Magnum trembled very slightly in his grasp; for a moment I thought I'd overdone it.

"We couldn't watch her twenty-four hours a day," he said. "So I figure Marcos got to her somehow. You got Marcos and the money. Now I got to shake it out of you."

"You play a nice one-string fiddle,"

191

I said. "But the tune gets pretty monotonous."

The lights changed and I gunned the car forward.

"We'll see, peeper," the big man said.

I turned again as he gestured with the muzzle of the Magnum. We were heading up one of the canyons now. The bungalows started thinning out. The street-lamps were left far behind when the gorilla signalled for the last time. I turned right on to a dirt road, the Buick's springs protesting. We drove up about two miles.

"This is as far as we go," the big man said.

I pulled the Buick up in front of a big frame bungalow that could have done with a lick of paint. There was nothing but a gravel drive in front and a lot knee-high in weeds. I killed the motor and the shrill chirring of cicadas flowed into the silence up here.

"You keep a nice place," I said.

The big man grunted.

"It suits us," he said.

There was a flare of yellow headlights. The scarlet Cadillac pulled in behind us.

"The gang's all here," I said.

I killed my own headlights and got out the Buick. The big man was backing out the other side. I pocketed thé Buick's keys while his eyes fractionally dropped to the ground. I didn't think he'd seen me. I stood and waited until the Cadillac's motor was switched off. Another man got out from behind the wheel. There was no one else. If the bungalow was empty that meant only two against one. I'd faced higher odds in the past.

The Cadillac's headlights were still switched on so I didn't try anything. The second man came round between me and the light. His face was away from the headlamps so I couldn't make it out at first. He moved over closer. He was tall, and so thin that his bones seemed to stick out from beneath his clothing in a way that was painful to look at.

He was dressed in a dark blue suit cut like a yachtsman's outfit, with vents in the back of the jacket. He wore a blue bow-tie that hung beneath his chin like a caricature of some nineteenth-century artist. He moved round to stand next to the big character. He had hair so blond that it was almost white. It was cut fairly close to his scalp and the breeze up here made it ripple like thistledown.

He had a dead white face with a livid red scar running from just below his right eye down toward the corner of his mouth. The stitching had slightly puckered that side of his face so that it looked like he was trying to smile. I found it slightly unnerving. Not that this character would be around long. Or rather, not that I would. I had no doubt what these boys were after.

When they realized I would be no use to them I would be strictly expendable. The thin man couldn't have been more than about thirty. He had red, fleshy lips that looked like another extension of the scar and his eyes were just blank black holes in his face. Definitely not a character to meet on a dark night; like tonight for instance. I grinned to myself.

It was the only amusement I had for the moment. The thin man passed his tongue across his lips.

"Do we get to do it here or inside?" he said.

"Here's as good as anywhere," the big man grunted. "No point in going inside. This won't take long."

"Suits me," the thin man said softly. "Do I get to take him?"

"Just a little more patience," the big man said. "I got some questions to ask him first."

The death's-head smiled.

"Just so long as it's understood. Harry's going to be a long time in hospital."

I looked at the big man. The Magnum was rock-steady in his hand.

"Did your friend bring his X-certificate with him?" I said. "I'll bet he's in great demand at Halloween."

The walking skeleton froze suddenly. A faint ripple seemed to pass through his frame.

"That man's dead," he said in a low, toneless voice.

"Sure, Gecko," the big man said uneasily. "But like I said we got to talk first."

He looked at me sharply.

"Lay off, will you? Gecko's sensitive."

I grinned.

"I thought you were in the rackets, not a ballet company."

The big man scowled. He took a step nearer to me. The Magnum came up, centred on my chest.

"Just take it easy," the big man repeated.

The character called Gecko stood motionless and stared at me. I knew then why he was called Gecko. I'd seen lizards sit on walls like that, remaining motionless for hours if need be. That way they caught flies and other insects. I decided I'd get in first if Gecko started anything. I don't tread on lizards normally but I'd make an exception in his case. The big man gestured with the Magnum.

"Over here."

I went and stood in front of the

headlights and waited. The big man looked around, like he was memorizing the terrain.

"We'd better get near the edge," he told the thin man. "Bring the car over and keep the headlamps on Faraday here."

The thin man slowly relaxed. He hadn't moved from the moment I'd spoken to him.

"Why waste time?" he said.

The big man grunted.

"Use your head, Gecko. You want to be rich, don't you?"

The skeleton shrugged.

"I get by all right."

The big man made an impatient, explosive noise deep down in his throat. He looked at the thin man like he was trying to explain something to a child. I noticed the Magnum barrel didn't move a fraction all the time he was talking to the other man.

"Just get behind the wheel and leave the thinking to me."

The thin man nodded.

"It's your show."

The big man inclined his head.

"Just so long as you remember that."

He gave me his full attention.

"Now, Mr Faraday, we'll just walk down a ways. Nothing fancy. I'll be right behind and I could drop you in seconds."

I smiled at him.

"But that wouldn't do you much good," I said. "You'd never get the money then."

The giant sighed.

"You're difficult to do business with, Faraday."

I walked on ahead of him, keeping my hands out from my sides.

"It's a difficult world," I told him. "Take my situation, for example. If I don't tell you about the money you kill me. If I do tell you then Gecko kills me. Where's the percentage?"

The big man shook his head. There was a slight flicker of irony in his eyes in the yellow beam from the headlights.

"It does seem unfair," he said. "But

that's the way we work. But there is a marginal benefit. You get out with less pain by co-operating."

"Great," I said.

The Cadillac's motor surged behind us and the headlamp beams brightened. I kept on walking. It had once been a garden here and there were the remains of pergolas and flower beds. The scrubby jungle through which we were moving must have been lawn. There was no cover in sight. As the yellow beams steadied up behind us, throwing the dark shadows of me and the big man on the grass, I could see it was going to be a difficult one.

I could hear the faint roar of the ocean now. We came out on to a broad shelf of rock. It was the edge of the cliff. My foot tapped against a small stone. It rattled across the scree and dropped outwards through undergrowth and presumably, into space beyond. I turned to face the big man. He smiled in the light from the main beams.

"This will do very nicely," he said.

15

THE red scar on Gecko's cheek puckered and twitched. It was like a wire pulling up the corner of his mouth. He stood near the edge of the drop with his long arms down at his sides. The clothing hung on his skeletal frame like it had been flung there by someone and had remained where it had fallen.

"Ready to start when you are," he told the big man softly.

The wrinkles at the corner of the big man's deep-set eyes made deep creases as he turned toward the thin character.

"For Christ's sake can't I get through to you? We want some information first."

The thin man watched me warily. He stood absolutely immobile.

"You won't get anything out of him by kindness," he said softly. "I know the type."

The big man ign[...] the Magnum slightl[...]

"Make it easy on [...] been tailing you. M[...] took it in turns."

The big man shool[...] tiently. He had iron-g[...] headlights of the car we[...]ing it to gold. It didn't make him look any easier to deal with.

"We followed you to Marcos' place. We hung around and saw you come out."

"You did a good job," I said. "I didn't see anyone."

The giant smiled thinly.

"When you got Gecko behind you you don't see him."

"I bet he's got his woodcraft badge too," I said.

Gecko didn't say anything but I could see a sort of ripple pass through his wiry frame. If I could keep needling him something might happen. That was the only way I would get a break tonight.

"Gecko kept tabs on you and I went in," the big man went on. "I found bath."

... my head.

... must have been a nasty shock

... ou."

The big man's mouth was an ugly gash.

"I'm used to death, Mr Faraday. But I must admit it was quite a financial shock. You went in and right after I found him dead. You must agree it looks bad. Who else could have had the money?"

"Search me," I said.

The giant scuffed with the toe of one big shoe in the long grass at his feet.

"You're just wasting time," Gecko said flatly.

I was getting tired of the record. It was time he changed to the flip side. The giant ignored him.

"What makes you think Marcos had the money?" I said. "If he had the money the girl would have been with him."

I looked toward him, screwing up my eyes against the glare from the headlights. The giant stared at me.

"You got a point," he said softly.

"My bet is the girl pulled out and took the money with her," I said.

Gecko smiled. This time he didn't bother to say anything. He was throwing surprises all the time.

"No good, Faraday," the big man said stolidly. "We already been through all that."

"All right," I said. "We'll slice it your way just for laughs. Larsen says Dale Holden couldn't have gotten out of L.A. without him knowing. It's possible but unlikely. She could have simply driven out by hire car any one of a hundred ways. And taken the money with her. It was in cash, remember. Which is pretty bulky stuff on that scale."

"On what scale?"

"Oh, come on," I said. "It was a hundred thousand dollars, wasn't it? It was no secret."

The big man shook his head.

"We heard different. It was pay-night. The figure was nearly two hundred thousand."

I didn't whistle but I felt like it.

"If there's one fact that's been given me straight on this case I've yet to hear it."

The red scar on Gecko's cheek twitched again.

"Maybe you just don't live right, Faraday," the big man said. "You got an honest face. That doesn't pay these days."

"Looks like it," I said. "But it just reinforces my point. Two hundred thousand would be twice as bulky as the first figure, even in high notes. There was no doubt it wasn't anywhere around Marcos's place."

"Maybe he put it in a bank deposit?" the big man said.

"Use your head," I told him. "That money was hot. Marcos wouldn't have used a bank. Banks want sums like that explained. You don't just roll up with suitcases."

"What's your suggestion?" Gecko said sullenly.

"I'm all out of suggestions," I said. "Besides, there wasn't anything in the apartment. Assuming he could have put the money in a safe deposit there was no sign of a slip. Whoever knocked over Marcos would have picked the place clean."

I could see doubt on the big man's face and I followed it up.

"We'd do better to join up and go halves," I said. "You know I haven't got it."

The big man was silent for another long moment. I could sense he was beginning to waver. Gecko still stood immobile; he was the dangerous one all right. Finally the big man shook his head. I could hear the shrill metallic sound of cicadas somewhere among the long grass.

"Anyone else but you I might have done a deal," the big man said. "You're too straight. We couldn't afford to let you go, anyway. You'd only tell Jack Larsen. And he wouldn't like our little side arrangement."

He cleared his throat as though the rasp in his voice was getting too much even for him.

"You know something. I still want that information."

I sighed.

"Just looks as though we shall have to do it the hard way."

The faintest flicker of a signal passed between the two men. While I was still blinking in the light of the headlamps and before I had time to dodge Gecko came dancing over toward me with incredible rapidity. His matchstick leg came round so fast it was just a blur in the yellow glare.

I ducked instinctively but I didn't quite make it. The edge of his shoe, like a sword-blade, came down on my shoulder and I felt numbing pain. I spun off and rolled toward the cliff edge. I let myself go when I saw what was underneath. There was a short limestone slope, ending on a broad ledge fringed with bushes. I slithered over the edge and went downward in a cloud of dust and small pebbles.

"You fool." the big man yelped. I could

hear his footsteps pounding toward the cliff. The man called Gecko came over and looked downward. His figure looked even more emaciated in the glare of the lamps.

"He's all right," he said contemptuously.

I kept my eyes half-closed. The big man had joined Gecko.

"No thanks to you," he told the thin man. "How the hell are we going to get him up now?"

"I can work on him down there," Gecko said. "It will save time."

"He looks to be out," the big man said. "I told you not to overdo it."

"You worry too much," Gecko said.

I was lying with my head and shoulders half in, half out of a clump of rough grass. I didn't move my legs and from above it must have looked pretty convincing. Fortunately it was only my left arm that was numb. I had the Smith-Wesson out the holster now. I put it carefully down in the grass in front of me. I looked downward. There was another ledge with small trees growing out of it. The cliff dropped sheer after that.

My fingers were scrabbling at the bottom of the canvas holster. I kept a spare clip for the Smith-Wesson there. Today there seemed to be only a single shell. Leastways, I couldn't feel any more. Unless the slugs had fallen out when I came down the cliff. I forced myself to keep my body still as I held the shell between my two longest fingers. I eased it out the holster, found I was sweating.

One shot was better than nothing. At least it gave me a chance. My biggest danger was if the big man decided he'd had enough. He could finish me from the cliff-top with the Magnum. Then all they'd have to do would be to push me over. I was relying on his greed to keep him working on me. No shot came but I was sweating plenty. I heard the rasp of a shoe on the rock then. I opened my eyes. Gecko was coming down the cliff-face, making heavy weather of it. Perhaps he had a fear of heights.

I had the shell now. I already had the

Smith-Wesson open. I eased the shell into the chamber, moved it into the firing position. I held the Smith-Wesson in my right hand, in among the thick grass. I had only the one shot. I had to make it count. My left arm and shoulder were throbbing nicely now.

I knew what I was going to do. It was pretty dim down here compared to the bluff up top. But if I miscalculated two bodies would go over the cliff instead of one. Gecko was hanging from a boulder with one hand, while his feet scrabbled for a hold. He'd come down the wrong way and had gotten into a steeper place.

"For Christ's sake," the big man grumbled. "Shake it up. This isn't the Matterhorn."

"It's easy enough from where you're standing," Gecko said.

His voice sounded as wobbly as his footing. "Perhaps you'd like to change places."

"You're getting your cut," the big man said. "Earn it."

The thin man swore. A few more

seconds passed. A hail of stones came down from the top of the cliff. I heard a faint cry of alarm, grinned crookedly to myself. I opened my eyes a little wider. The man Gecko was hanging by one hand from a limestone ledge. His feet were only about six feet above the ground but the taut, paralysed attitude of his body told me it might just as well have been the North Face of the Eiger.

There would never be a better opportunity. It was him or me. The big man had gone forward. He was bending on one knee, giving advice to Gecko. I shifted slightly in the grass and took careful aim. The crack of the explosion stung my ear-drums and powder-smoke was thick in my nostrils. The bright red flame from the muzzle seemed to light up the darkness of the cliff-top.

The big man had gone over backwards at the shot, flattening himself on the ground. Gecko's body slammed inward toward the cliff. He stayed there like he was pinned to the stonework; then he was coming unglued, his body relaxing.

He fell, his arms and legs limp; I knew he was a dead man then.

I was up on my feet; I'd chosen my spot as carefully as possible. The Smith-Wesson was useless now. I had to make it look good. Gecko's body hit the ground near me and buckled forward. I moved back slightly and took the shock of the collision. Then I threw myself backward and shouted. I could see the shadow of the big man at the cliff-top.

Gecko and I went down in a tangle of arms and legs. I hoped it looked realistic. It felt like it to me. I sensed the cliff edge fall away beneath me, held tight to the thin man. Then we both went over the lip of the drop together.

16

THE fall was longer than I thought. For one sickening moment I thought I'd miscalculated. I let go the thin man, felt branches whipping past my face. One of them drew blood. I hit scree and rolled over. The thin man's body went crashing on beyond the secondary ledge. I kept on rolling; I dug in my heels and scrabbled with my hands. My speed was decreasing very slowly. In a few more seconds I'd run out of ledge.

My feet struck the edge, went into space. The strain on my wrists as I caught the saplings almost dislocated my spine. There was a roaring in my ears and I tasted blood. The crashing of Gecko's body through the branches went on. He seemed to take an age to fall. Then I was swinging gently, only half conscious. There was an enormous silence. Slowly the sounds of the night came soaking back in; the shrill chirp of cicadas; the faint beat of surf from far away.

Perspiration was pouring off me; I could feel my shirt sticking to my back. In my throat was the sour smell of fear. I'd almost loused the whole thing up; I'd been within an ace of going over the cliff myself. My fall had been completely uncontrolled the last few yards. I was thinking peculiar things too. The Smith-Wesson for example.

Had I or had I not put it back in the harness before I went over? It didn't matter a damn really but it seemed important to know, situated as I was. It had been with me through the years and it had gotten me out of more tight corners than I could remember. I recollected then; I'd put it back before Gecko had come down the bluff at me. I could feel its weight against my chest as I dangled there.

I opened my eyes, looked at the saplings; they seemed pretty frail. I hoped to God their roots wouldn't tear out with my weight. Though if they hadn't gone when I grabbed them the chances were they wouldn't go now. I could feel something trickling down my wrist; sweat or blood, maybe. A yellow light flashed across the rough ground. I closed my eyes. I wondered if the cliff overhang would prevent me getting back up.

Then I opened my lids again. The light couldn't have been a car headlamp. I was nowhere near a road. My mind suddenly clicked into focus. The beam of the torch went on probing. My head and shoulders were protected by the foliage but if the big man came down the cliff to look for me and Gecko he might see my wrists at the base of the saplings.

I hung, conscious of the aching strain on my arms now, and watched the yellow disc of dancing torch-light glide from bush to bush. The big man was coming down the bluff by the easier path. I'd lost sight of him because he'd gotten on to the level of the first ledge. I hoped he'd be quick about it; I didn't want to hang around here all night. I grinned crookedly to myself.

That was when I felt an increase in the flow of blood on my left wrist. I took my eyes off the torchlight that was dancing over the bushes above me and focused them on my wrist. I couldn't see anything for a minute. Then the torch-light came nearer, steadied up. The big man was examining the ground of the ledge above me, inch by inch, moving the torch across the terrain to make a box search.

A shadow crawled at the corner of my eye. The faint irritation in my left wrist went on. It was an itch now. I longed to let go with my right and scratch it. But I knew that would be fatal so I stayed put. There was a grating noise on scree as the big man gained the cliff edge above me. He swore to himself and a thin stream of small stones went rattling down the face. I grinned again. I fancied it was a little more crooked this time. My shoulders were beginning to ache.

The big man's shoe grated on the ground. I looked up. The torch-light was bobbing about, quite close to the edge. I hoped there would be a nice broad trail in the dust leading directly to the drop. I knew Gecko had made quite a hole in the branches and undergrowth as he went through. The beam had steadied up, like the man up top was examining something.

I felt the strange sensation in my wrist again. I looked across toward it. The light was brighter now that the big man was closer to me, the torch beam stationary. There was too much light really. It showed up the stems of the grass and the roots of the saplings I was holding on to. That was when I saw the big grey snake moving slowly across my wrist.

If I'd been sweating before perspiration was pouring off me now. I clenched my teeth, all the pains in my arms forgotten. The snake was moving across my wrist in rippling waves but so slowly it seemed like it was stationary.

Strangely enough its touch was dry and brittle; I'd read somewhere that snakes weren't slimy but I didn't want it proved this way. I heard a grating noise then and looked up.

The yellow beam of the torch danced across the grass and the stems of the saplings and steadied. The big man came and stood about a yard away from me. I hoped to Christ he wouldn't make any sudden movement to alarm the snake.

I risked another glance at it. It was still moving across. I couldn't see its head; it was probably in the grass somewhere near the big man's feet. It was too much to hope that it would bite him. I'd been lucky once tonight. It wouldn't happen again. I guessed the snake had been sleeping or doing whatever snakes do farther down, perhaps beneath the roots of the saplings. It had been disturbed by Gecko's body crashing through and was making its way upward to safety.

I got my head in as tight to the grass stems as I could and hoped that the big man wouldn't look directly downward. Surely he couldn't fail to see me if he did. He stood there for what seemed like a year. He was so close I could hear him muttering something to himself. The torch beam wavered a little and moved slowly away. But the big man was still standing in the same position like he was looking over the L.A. basin, admiring the view.

I risked another glance at the thing on my wrist. I'd forgotten the itching momentarily but it was back again now. The snake had grey stripes on a darkish background. I couldn't remember whether that was lethal or not. Most snakes in California are poisonous but there are some harmless ones. It wasn't a rattler. That was something to be thankful for.

The glistening band of striped skin went its deliberate way; it was a lot thinner now. That meant the head was away from me and the tail should be coming up. I was conscious again of the intolerable ache in my back and the throbbing in my wrists; I was hanging straight down with my heels in space and a trembling fit was beginning to pass through my body.

The torch beam moved again; I held my breath. The big man was moving back from the edge a little. I heard his boot scrape on rock. Then the aimless circling of the cone of light recommenced. He quartered the ground for a minute or so. Sweat was blinding me, trickling down my forehead into my eyes. A tiny whiplash was moving across my wrist now. The tip flickered off almost reluctantly and I heard the faint movement in the grass.

A few moments later the torch beam was suddenly directed at the ground; I heard the hissed intake of breath. I tried the last twisted smile of the evening. The light wobbled so much I thought the torch was going to drop to the ground. The big man had found the snake.

"Mother of God!" I heard him say in a trembling voice.

What with me and Gecko it had been a pretty hectic evening for him. The snake was the clincher. I heard the almost hysterical way his boots were scrabbling back up the face of the cliff the way he'd come down. I hoped I would have enough strength to haul myself back up. And that I wouldn't meet the snake again.

I stayed where I was, conscious of the heavy strain on my muscles. My wrists were numb and I could see blood trickling from under my finder-nails. I was drenched in perspiration; it trickled down my face, penetrating my collar and turning my shirt into a limp rag. I seemed to have been here between the sea and the sky for years. Worse still, there was a trembling spasm that seemed to start in the pit of my stomach and work its way upwards.

I could hear the big man scrabbling away. Pebbles and masses of scree were coming down the cliff-face on to the ledge above. Half a century seemed to go by; it was probably all of thirty seconds. I couldn't wait for the big man to go away. I had to risk it. If I left it any longer I wouldn't be able to make it.

I was shocked to find how feeble I felt when I started to put pressure on the saplings to lift myself.

I came back down to the full extent of my arms, sweat bursting out all over. I heard the first cough of the motor then. The headlights of the car blinked and started reversing from the cliff edge. I wondered what the big man would do about the scarlet Caddy Gecko had been driving. Noise didn't matter now. I kicked with my legs, found my right shoe jammed against a root or something. I tested it, found it held.

I almost screamed with pain when I took the weight off my arms. I sagged forward, fighting for breath. It was easier now. I kicked upward, finding a fresh hold in the branches for my numbed and bleeding hands. Somehow, using hands and feet, I dragged myself up through the roots and the grass, found firm ground beneath my knees.

The motor gunned up on the cliff top above and I heard the automobile go roaring back along the track in the ruined garden of the bungalow. I got up, found I could stand. I dragged myself forward, making a big detour to avoid the ground where I thought the snake might be. The yellow beam of the headlights died out overhead. The faint whisper of the car engine ceased and I was alone with the wind, the sky and the distant murmur of the sea.

It took me a quarter of an hour to get up the short distance to the top of the cliff. I'd probably chosen the more difficult way. Or maybe I was more beat up than I thought. When I hit the plateau I found the Cadillac where Gecko had left it. The Buick was still in front of the big frame bungalow. I shuffled my way through the knee-high weeds feeling like a little old gentleman of eighty-five. Correction. A little old gentleman of eighty-five would probably have been far fitter.

I found the car keys in my pocket where I'd put them and got behind the wheel of the Buick. Another fit of trembling came over me when I lit a cigarette. I feathered out the smoke. I daren't look in the rear mirror. I was afraid of what I might see. I got out the Buick quickly, dropped the cigarette into the grass. The ground came up to meet me as I leaned over and vomited like a dog.

17

I LOOKED at my watch. Incredibly, it was still going. I put it to my ear to make sure. It was only nine o'clock in the evening. It seemed like three years since I'd gone to pick up the Buick in the garage. I pulled up at an intersection as the lights changed to red and idled the motor. I caught a glimpse of myself in the mirror. I looked almost normal. I'd cleaned myself up a little on the bluff before I left.

Apart from a few cuts and bruises sustained when I went over the cliff I was all in one piece. Except that my arms ached like hell still. My clothing and shoes still looked dusty but there was little I could do about that until I got home. That could wait anyway. I wasn't going to eat at Dave Chasen's. I'd gone over the Cadillac. I soon saw why the big man had left it. It had been stolen if the name and address on the licence details was anything to go by.

I changed gear again and crossed the intersection, turning left to a boulevard where there were some shops and restaurants. I went in a cafeteria and got outside a coffee and sandwich. Then I went in the toilet and washed my hands and tidied myself up. By the time I came out I was almost normal. Then I drove over to my rented house on Park West. I phoned Stella at home but there was no reply.

I broke out some more shells for the Smith-Wesson from the small armoury I keep in a locked cupboard in my bedroom and reloaded. I felt better then. I checked on the gas and turned the Buick back down the hill. It was after ten when I hit Ticonderoga Drive. I eased over into the lane bordered by the ubiquitous palms and pulled up in front of the tall iron gates between the stone pillars. They were locked but there was a light in the white stucco lodge with the green Spanish tiles. I left the motor running and got out and thumbed the buzzer set in the right-hand pillar.

A metallic voice came out the steel grille set into the pillar.

"Yeah?"

"Mike Faraday to see Jack Larsen."

"You expected?"

The voice was laconic, incurious.

"He'll see me any time," I said.

"Right," the speaker spat.

It froze into silence. I waited, watching an oblong of yellow that was the lodge doorway growing wider. The dim form of the big man with the gut materialized from the shadows. Simon came forward and gave me a long, hard stare through the grille-work.

"You must have a pretty good reason for calling so late," he said.

I nodded.

"I have," I told him. "I just about wrapped up this case."

The big man grunted. He was unlocking the gate. He swung it wide.

"That'll please Mr Larsen," he said. "You got a line on the girl?"

"I think so," I said. "She's not far away from here right now."

The big man's eyebrows went up.

"That so? It's good news to hear."

"She owe you money too?" I said.

He grinned. He shook his head.

"Naw. But anything that will get the sourness out of the characters around here has my vote. DaVinci came back in about half hour ago. He was real sore."

"Leonardo?" I said. "Big man with a face like hammered glass?"

The gateman grinned again.

"That's him. You want for me to announce you?"

I shook my head.

"Do me a favour. Let it go this once. I've got something to settle with him."

The gateman shrugged.

"Sure. Anything to oblige. I got no reason to feel grateful to the big guy for anything. If I told you half the things that went on around here . . ."

He was unlocking the other half of the gate. I went back to the Buick and drove up inside the gates. I killed the motor and got out and waited while the big man relocked them behind me.

"You wouldn't be using the phone after I've gone?" I said. "It would kinda spoil the surprise."

The big man shook his head. He took the bill from my fingers and stuffed it back into the top pocket of my jacket.

"I could take offence at that, mister," he said evenly. "But I'm a pretty nice guy."

"Sure," I said. "Just so long as we know where we stand."

He opened his mouth as if to say something but we were suddenly interrupted by a low coughing sound which seemed to come from far off among the trees.

"That's another point," he said. "The lights will be on at the top of the steps. There's things loose in the grounds so for Christ's sake don't go fooling around."

I gave him a long look.

"What sort of things?"

"Wild animals," he said. "Get up the steps quick and keep in the light. They won't come up there. They stick to the dark places."

"Thanks," I said. "Like I said before it's a real nice setup."

The big man's face shone with perspiration beneath the black curly hair. He still wore the jeans tucked into top-boots. The black leather belt had difficulty in holding his enormous bulk in. He wasn't really fat, just massive. I wouldn't have liked to try anything with him. Jack Larsen knew how to pick his guards all right. The big man must have guessed what I was thinking.

"Never came across a man so frightened of his life as Jack Larsen," he said simply. "For a guy who's cut himself a piece of every racket in the book it's pathetic."

"Plenty of enemies?" I said.

The big man nodded.

"That's why he doesn't go out often these days."

"The poor son-of-a-bitch," I said softly.

The big man's eyes were hard and burning now.

"Don't waste any sympathy on him, Mr Faraday. Remember what I said now. No fooling around in the dark."

"You must be joking," I said. "I'd drive the car up the steps if I could."

He stepped back. I got in the car and started her up the long drive with its curious right-angles.

The Smith-Wesson made a hard knot against my chest muscles as I tooled the Buick round the bends, the yellow headlamp beams stencilling harsh shadows across the tarmac. The foliage stood out sharp and clear, each leaf and stem looking like a solarized photograph in the harsh light. I kept the car in low gear, keeping a close eye on the roadside. There was no way the big man could know I'd missed going over the cliff but I wanted to make sure of surprising him.

The perfume of tropical flowers and fresh-cut grass made an agreeable aroma in the nostrils. You're not here for the gardening notes, Faraday, I told myself. I was almost up the end of the approach road now and I put my foot down a little as I got to another straight.

A great black shadow swooped low over the nose of the car, kept on going. I'd ducked instinctively and reached for the Smith-Wesson with my disengaged hand. There was a crashing in the undergrowth and a snarling noise. One of Jack Larsen's pets, evidently. I tried to remember what the gateman had told me on my original visit.

I could hear a heavy body crackling in the bushes at the roadside. It was effortlessly keeping pace with the car. The gateman hadn't been exaggerating. I tried to kid myself I was angry when I felt my hand tremble slightly on the Smith-Wesson butt. I knew it was fear, though. I'd been caught out and I was sore at myself as well; if the big man had been at the roadside he couldn't have failed to drop me.

I was nearly up to the steps now and there was nothing but smooth open roadway between myself and the nearest fringe of ornamental bushes. I pulled up at the foot of the steps and killed the motor. The silence crowded back in. Except that it wasn't complete silence. There was a faint rumbling noise coming from the edge of the driveway about twenty yards back.

It was the sort of rumbling a bull mastiff makes when it's angry; or, not to put the analogy too high, the kind of noise you hear at a zoo. In the big cat house, for example. It set a nerve squeaking in my spine somewhere. I had to force myself to get out the car. I moved over and got out on the side nearest the steps, keeping the Buick between me and the driveway edge.

There was a faint snarl now. I had the Smith-Wesson out, the barrel held steadily toward the bushes. I could feel sweat trickling heavily down my shirt. All my face was a mask of perspiration. I started walking backwards, very slowly, up the flight of steps. It was quite light here, because there was a lamp at the top, but I felt like I was alone

232

in the universe. It must have been a crazy sight if anyone had been there to see.

A grown man, edging up backward, step by step, feeling for the next tread with hesitant feet. But I had a feeling that if I'd turned my back on whatever was there in the bushes, it would have been on me in two or three powerful strides. And if it had broken cover I would have dropped the revolver and run. Which would have been fatal under the circumstances.

About a year passed and I was more than halfway up the steps now and well within the cone of light. The growling had stopped but I kept on going in the same manner until I judged the immediate danger was over. I had to consider that the thing, whatever it was, might circle around, so I didn't relax until I was up on the terrace. There were a lot of lights coming from the house and spilling on to the lawn. I put the gun away then and went over toward the French windows. I had no intention of announcing myself this evening.

I went on down the terrace, keeping in the heavy shadows of the trees. There was a radio or TV blaring out music somewhere which covered the faint sound my feet made on the flag-stones. I wanted to make sure how many staff were around before I went on in. I had a score to settle and it wouldn't wait. I looked through several of the lighted windows.

There were three women and a Filipino houseboy on this side of the building so far as I could make out. Nobody to provide any heavy opposition. I didn't know how many other heavies Larsen kept on the premises. I had a feeling that tonight would wrap up the case. Don't ask me how I knew. I was no farther forward in figuring out what had happened to Dale Holden or who'd killed Marcos than when I'd started out. Except that it was all tied up with this house. It had begun here and it would end here; I felt that way down in my entrails.

I finished staring through windows and went back up along the terrace, looking for the entrance I'd used with Lauritzen on my previous visits. I skirted the heart-shaped swimpool. Lights were glistening and breaking into a million splinters on its surface. I looked at them thoughtfully. The patterns they made were just as enigmatic as everything else about Jack Larsen's problem.

I found the set of glass doors I'd used on the other two occasions. I only visited Larsen's place three times in all and I never ever used the front door. That was curious too, come to think of it. The doors were unlocked. I opened one a crack and listened. I could hear voices coming from a short way away. I opened the window wide and went on in.

I stopped just inside the door. The place was the library where I'd been before. This time it was occupied. There were book stacks jutting out a little way along. The voices were coming from beyond that. I eased my way down a little, keeping on the thick carpet. Despite the heat of the evening there was a fire smouldering in the big stone fireplace up at the far end.

There were two big wing chairs either side of the fire I could see as I eased round the end of the stack. Two equally big feet were protruding from the chair with its back toward me. Jack Larsen sat in the other, facing me obliquely. His eyes were intent on the man in the chair opposite and he hadn't seen me. I went back down the stack. I took two big leather-bound volumes out of a shelf at eye level. I could see over the top of the books on the other side of the stack while remaining in shadow.

Jack Larsen wore a red silk dressing gown over a white shirt with a black bow-tie. Maybe he was going out to dinner; or perhaps he had not long come in. There was a fragrant smell of cigar smoke in the air mingling with the heavy scent of resin from the smouldering logs in the fireplace. Larsen's legs, in black trousers and ending in brightly polished evening shoes, extended only halfway down the wing-chair. A footstool had been placed underneath and he rested his feet on this.

There was a brief lull in the conversation but I'd gathered from the tone when I came in earlier that there was something acrimonious in the discussion. Larsen's glossy black hair shone under the lamps and the thick smoke from the cigar between his fingers went up in a lazy plume toward the high ceiling. His sandy eye-lashes were half over the strange black pupils of his eyes and his thin lips were compressed.

He had an orange juice with chunks of ice floating in the heavy frosted glass at his elbow. The silence was like that of an interval between two claps of thunder. Then Larsen opened his eyes. His voice cracked like a whip.

"You've failed!" he said contemptuously.

The voice sounded like a buzz-saw

grating through sandstone tonight.

"I did my best," the man with his back to me said. I recognized the voice now. It was Joey all right. I got out the Smith-Wesson and threw off the safety-catch. Then I put it down on a small occasional table near my right hand. I bent to the gap between the books again.

"Your best is hardly adequate," Larsen went on. "I appear to be surrounded by fools and incompetents."

"You get what you pay for," the big man called Joey said. "Simon said the girl took her heap. She could have got clear out of town."

Larsen shook his head. His eyes were burning as he fixed them on the big man opposite.

"I thought I'd made it quite clear. We knew within half an hour. All the exits were covered. The private army as well as our own people. There were road-blocks, remember?"

"Sure," said DaVinci reluctantly. "You got the organization, Mr Larsen. I give you that. But there are ways of leaving town . . . "

Larsen shook his head impatiently. Little spots of red were showing on his cheeks now.

"A child could understand it," he said softly. "She's got to be here in town. That's why I hired Faraday."

"He hasn't come up with anything," the big man said sullenly. "And Harry . . . "

"Harry's still in hospital." Larsen said mildly.

He smiled suddenly. It briefly transformed his face.

"Faraday's got brains as well as guts. If anyone can find her he will."

I picked up the Smith-Wesson and eased out from behind the book-stack.

"Sure," I said. "But first Leonardo and I have a little business to settle."

There was a deep silence. Larsen didn't seem at all put out. He looked up at me with a continuation of his earlier smile.

"Good evening, Mr Faraday. I'd prefer you to ring in the usual manner, but you are none the less welcome."

The big man got up out the chair with a face like death. The cannon that had suddenly grown in his hand seemed as big as the mouth of the freeway tunnel.

18

I LOOKED at Joey.

"I wouldn't if I were you," I said. "It's even Steven."

DaVinci seemed to notice the Smith-Wesson for the first time.

"We got to talk," he said thickly.

"Sure," I said. "I just came here for that purpose."

The midget seemed non-plussed. He turned his dark eyes quizzically on the big man.

"Put it away," he said softly. "What the hell's the matter with you?"

"Leonardo here is a little jittery tonight," I said. "He tried to bounce me over a cliff earlier on."

The big man's face looked as shapeless as putty. A glaze of sweat had broken out on it. He swallowed once or twice, found he couldn't get his words out. Larsen looked evenly at the big man. He didn't move from the chair.

"Did you, Joey?"

DaVinci swallowed again. He got some words out in the end. The gun barrel was pointing at the floor now. I relaxed my finger on the Smith-Wesson trigger and lowered it fractionally.

"I don't know what he's talking about, Mr Larsen," Joey said.

Larsen looked inquiringly at me. He was taking in my somewhat battered appearance now.

"It seems to be your turn, Mr Faraday."

"Joey's just being bashful," I said. "He had a character called Gecko with him. I had to kill him."

Larsen moistened his lips with his tongue and reached out for his glass of orange juice. His nerves were admirably steady tonight.

"I'm listening, Mr Faraday."

Both of us ignored the big man, who stood like a bronze statue in the middle of the carpet, halfway between the two wing chairs. I kept a pretty sharp eye on his gun-hand though.

"It was quite simple, Mr Larsen," I said. "They were trying to shake me down. I went to Marcos' place. I found him dead in his bath. The two men thought I'd got your two hundred thousand. It was two hundred grand, wasn't it? I believe you made a slight error when you were giving me the amount. But it's understandable when one is dealing with those sort of figures."

"Quite," said Larsen smoothly. "It was a quarter of a million if you must know. In high denomination notes. It was pay-night, you understand. I had to be away. I made the mistake of trusting the pay-out to Dale."

"It was an expensive mistake," I said. "And as we decided earlier, too tricky for the police to handle."

Larsen nodded affably. His eyes were thoughtful as he looked at DaVinci from under his sandy lashes.

"Joey was trying to cross you," I said. "He tried to make a deal with me. When that failed he hoped to beat it out of me. I took a chance and went over the cliff."

Larsen smiled briefly but his dead eyes were icy as he continued to stare at Joey.

"I hope you have some logical explanation, Joey," he said gently. "It may be difficult otherwise."

He turned his gaze on to me again.

"Dear, dear, Mr Faraday. You seem to have had a rough evening. But you are remarkably durable. I am glad to see my trust was not misplaced."

"I'm the only person around here who can be trusted," I said.

The midget permitted himself another smile, this time about three millimetres wide.

"You may well be right, Mr Faraday."

He put down his glass and fumbled in the cushion at his side. The big man came out of his trance then. He half-raised the gun. I brought the Smith-Wesson up again. Joey was white around the mouth.

Are you going to believe this baboon or me?" he said.

Larsen drew his lips together in a wry, jagged line.

"There's no question of who I believe," he said. "A very good thousand dollars' worth. Mr Faraday wins hands down."

Joey shifted uneasily on the carpet, turning slightly to look at Larsen. The big man seemed diminished, not so hard and durable. Even his voice was no longer like rusted metal. He held the Magnum loosely, its barrel turned halfway between me and Larsen.

"Can't you see what he's trying to do, boss?" he asked. "He's trying to get between us."

Larsen smiled briefly.

"He's doing rather well," he said. "Though we were never that close. I expect some degree of graft in my employees. I allow for that. About ten per cent is usually permissible. But a quarter of a million is plain theft."

His black eyes were very hard now, beneath the sandy lashes.

"That I cannot tolerate," he said.

DaVinci laughed deep down in his

throat. He took a step toward me.

"Just give me a minute," he said. "I can prove he's lying."

Larsen shook his head. The big man couldn't see his expression because he had his back to the midget now. He brought the Magnum up. I stepped back behind the bookcase, raising the Smith-Wesson. I miscalculated badly. I caught the muzzle beneath one of the shelves; the pain as the heavy wood gashed my knuckles made me relax my grip. I opened my fingers and the gun bounced to the floor.

I could see the triumph in DaVinci's eyes as he came forward, raising the Magnum. The explosion made an absurdly trivial pop in the silence of the library.

DaVinci changed expression. The light died out of his eyes. He took two stiff steps forward. He jerked as the popping noise sounded again. The barrel of the Magnum was sagging toward the carpet now. It dropped as scarlet spread from the big man's mouth. The gun exploded as it hit the library floor; I got back behind the shelf as the heavy bullet went ricochetting away among the books. Several volumes flew about the room. A rain of paper came down toward the floor, hanging thickly in the air like snow.

Larsen was on his feet; he was so tiny it still looked like he was sitting. DaVinci was going down, an incredulous expression on his hammered metal face. Thin wisps of blue smoke grew from the barrel of the pistol Larsen had taken from behind the cushion of his chair.

DaVinci demolished a table as he went down. Vases and a bowl of flowers went rolling over the floor. The big man gurgled once or twice and then found he was dead. His legs gave a last convulsive twitch and were still.

I got up, still hearing the thunder of the explosion and tasting powder-smoke. Larsen stood looking down at the big man without any expression on his tanned face.

"Disloyalty is something I cannot stand," he said softly.

"I know how you feel," I said. "And thanks."

Larsen smiled thinly.

"I did not do it for your benefit, Mr Faraday."

I got out a handkerchief and bound it round my gashed hand; my knuckles were bleeding nicely now. I bent down to pick up the Smith-Wesson.

"I shouldn't do that if I were you, Mr Faraday," Larsen said quickly. "This gun holds three more. Plenty in case of further emergency."

I shrugged.

"Just as you wish. Though what other emergencies were you expecting?"

Larsen smiled again.

"The evening is young yet, Mr Faraday. And I find that one weapon in a room is enough. It may lead to accidents otherwise."

He was still looking down at the big man's body. Then he shifted his gaze back to me.

"You were speaking the truth?"

"Sure I was speaking the truth." I told

him. "It happened like I said."

He nodded thoughtfully. He scratched his chin with the barrel of the gun. I stepped over toward the telephone which was on a low table halfway between and to one side of the two wing chairs.

"Oughtn't we to get some law in?" I said.

Larsen got forward between me and the telephone as quickly as a striking snake. He was so tiny I had to look almost down to my toe-caps to study his expression properly.

"No law, Mr Faraday," he said. "I thought I'd made it quite clear. If I can't afford the police over the missing money, how can I ask their help over a corpse on my library floor?"

"That's your problem," I said. "Or are you just going to wait for the garbage men?"

There were red spots on Larsen's cheeks now.

"He will be disposed of," he said. "Just leave it to me."

I took another step toward him.

"I have to report it," I said. "You're forgetting my position."

An irritable expression flitted across the little man's features.

"I haven't forgotten your position, Mr Faraday. Which makes the whole thing very regrettable. Especially as you'd come up here to tell me something about Dale. Or have I misread your presence here?"

I shook my head.

"You haven't misread anything, Mr Larsen. I've been giving your problem a lot of thought. It's my guess Dale Holden never left this place."

There was an ugly silence. Larsen's dark eyes turned to search my face.

"You'd better make yourself plain, Mr Faraday," he said softly.

I shook my head.

"I aim to, Mr Larsen. Figure it out for yourself. No-one's come up with anything since the gateman saw her drive off. She can't have vanished into thin air."

Larsen shrugged. He held the pistol down at his side and frowned at it like it had the answers to all the problems in the dark circle of its barrel.

"This is your department, Mr Faraday. What are you getting at?"

"I've been working on this thing for days. I haven't come up with anything concrete. Except that Dale Holden disappeared. And with her went a good deal of your money. Or what nominally passes for your money."

Jack Larsen's eyes flickered momentarily but he didn't say anything. I went over and sat down on an arm of the wing chair and stared at the thing that was lying on the floor.

"So far I haven't met anybody on this case who wasn't lying to me. Either everyone's got a motive for concealing the true circumstances or this is just normal in your sort of world."

Jack Larsen went back over to sit down in his wing chair again. He fixed his eyes on the low flames in the fireplace.

"You still haven't got to the point, Mr Faraday."

"Someone in your household knows

something, Mr Larsen," I said. "You got a lot of curious people around. Apart from the plug-uglies, that is. Mr Lauritzen, for example . . . "

I stopped. Larsen got up quickly, an alert expression on his face.

"Stay here," he said urgently.

He went over behind my chair. I looked around. He was standing by the half-open room door. I measured the distance between the chair where I was sitting and the Smith-Wesson. It was too far. I stayed put and waited for him to come back. He reappeared silently in front of me and resumed his seat. He grunted and picked up his glass of orange juice. He drained it noisily.

"I thought I heard something," he said. "We don't want to disturb the staff."

"Sure," I said. "They must be used to the sound of gunfire."

Larsen shook his head.

"They can't hear from there," he said harshly. "Besides, they always have the TV on full blast. You were saying?"

"Dale Holden," I said. "Supposing she

had a friend on the staff. Supposing she came back in, hiding in the boot of someone's car for example?"

Larsen's eyes flickered. His face had a strange, almost bestial expression. He got up and started pacing around with tense, nervous strides. He stopped to face me.

"You can't be serious, Mr Faraday."

"I can't prove it, if that's what you mean," I said. "But it's the conclusion I've been forced back on this last few hours. I may be wrong, of course. But it's my bet she never left here. If she did then someone within this house and grounds knows what's happened to her."

Larsen's eyes had an expression that was far away. His lips were drawn into the tight gash I'd come to know so well. He stood silently for almost thirty seconds, his eyes searching some impossible distance.

"Hiding out at the centre of the storm," he breathed. "Yes, it has a touch of genius, Mr Faraday."

He took a step toward me and looked up at me searchingly. He still had to look up even when I was sitting down.

"You're something of a genius yourself, Mr Faraday."

"If I'm right," I said.

Larsen sat down on the edge of the wing-chair and cradled the pistol on his lap.

"You're right, Mr Faraday," he said heavily. "I must think about this."

"That means the money's here," I said. "Where safer?"

Larsen gave me a crooked smile. His face was very ugly at that moment.

"I shall have to think about that too," he said.

His face had a strange expression as he glanced at me.

"A pity, really, Mr Faraday. You were about the only person who ever levelled with me. And you really earned your thousand dollars."

"What do you mean?" I said

Larsen frowned as though I'd said something obtuse.

"It's obvious, Mr Faraday, isn't it? I brought you in because I couldn't afford to have the police nosing into my affairs. I can afford it even less now with Joey here on the floor."

He shook his head slowly.

"No, Mr Faraday. In for a penny in for a pound. Get up."

I did like he said. There didn't seem any percentage in not doing so. The gun was directed steadily on my gut.

"What do we do now?" I said. "Shoot me here or in the garden?"

Larsen looked at me almost absently.

"I'll think of something, Mr Faraday. But there's no sense in ruining the carpet further. The grounds would be more appropriate. I'm sure I can arrange a suitable accident."

"For all your money you're a fool," I said. "Joey would have killed me if you hadn't stopped him. With me as a witness you're in the clear."

Larsen shook his head again. There was regret in his eyes.

"There is a lot in what you say, Mr Faraday. But that would involve a great many things I dread. Police investigations, newspaper publicity. And there are my other affairs that would come to light. I think not."

My eyes flickered over the Smith-Wesson as we got up close. There was no possibility of getting to it. Larsen was right behind me.

"It's your funeral, Larsen," I said.

I turned at the other side of the book stack and faced him. The midget smiled ironically.

"On the contrary, it's your funeral, Mr Faraday," he corrected me.

We were up near the French windows now. I moved to one side as Larsen went to open them. The gun was framed steadily on my midriff. Larsen had the windows open. He flung them wide. I looked out into the grounds. There was nothing but a great blackness beyond the terrace.

Something of the darkness detached itself. It came like a black, murderous streak through the silence. I flung myself to the floor as Larsen's gun blammed twice.

19

A HIGH, screaming noise seemed to scald the nerves. Plaster rained from the ceiling, making a choking white mist. I rolled over and coughed. Larsen was on the floor, a limp figure, silent now, being shaken like a rag doll. A low, worrying noise mingled with the sound of cracking bones. I dragged myself away into the shadow of a bookstack.

The head of the black panther looked like something out of a horror movie as it paused over Larsen's body. Its sensitive ears twitched as they heard the faint sound from the terrace. The yellow eyes glowed; there was red round the muzzle. I tried to screw myself up into as small a ball as possible. I looked around for the Smith-Wesson, couldn't see it.

The panther growled. It whirled quickly, its claws making sharp scraping noises on the parquet. The face of the big man looked in at the window. The heavy whip cracked through the air. The massive form looked as big as a house as he came in with quick, confident strides.

He hardly glanced at the thing that had been Jack Larsen. He kicked the gun away. It skidded over the floor. The panther snarled, raising itself on its hind legs. The whip cracked again. The big man drove it toward the French doors.

"Back, Sheba!"

The great black form melted into the deeper blackness outside. The gateman called Simon came over and looked down at me dispassionately.

"I suppose I ought to thank you," I said. "But did you have to do that?"

I got to my feet, brushed myself down. I pointed over toward Larsen. The big man shrugged.

"He had it coming," he said. "When I saw him at the window it seemed as good a time as any. So I slipped Sheba."

"You saved my life, anyway," I said.

Simon had a strange smile on his face. The muzzle of the gun in his hand was still turned toward me.

"We'll see, Mr Faraday," he said. "You was pretty smart back there, making believe you'd cracked the case. I had to come up and find out for myself."

I shook my head.

"It was only the vaguest suspicion. I figured the girl had never gotten out of the estate. That was true wasn't it?"

The big man swallowed. He looked down and avoided my eye. Something wet rolled down his cheek. My face must have looked as astonished as I felt.

"Dale Holden was my wife, Mr Faraday."

He looked over toward Larsen again.

"I had to do it, you see. The whole works came apart. Nothing went to schedule the way we planned it."

I got out my package of cigarettes and offered him one. He took it, then backed away, lighting it with a lighter he took out his pants pocket. He had on

259

a blue windcheater now and he looked even bigger than when I'd seen him earlier. I lit my own cigarette and put the match-stalk down in an onyx tray on a table near the door.

"What about the panther?" I said. "Won't it come back?"

Simon shook his head.

"I got her well trained. It was opportune, that's all. Larsen kicked her once or twice when she was chained up. She never forgot it."

I walked back toward the library door and drew the curtains. It was very quiet now and I could hear the faint fret of wind outside the windows.

"You seem remarkably self-possessed," I said.

I glanced from Larsen's body to that of Joey up near the fireplace. The place looked like the last act of Hamlet. Simon grinned crookedly.

"Nothing else matters any more, Mr Faraday. I'd just like to tell it straight. It's not important, being only you. But I'd like someone to know."

I didn't get the last remark but I didn't think it wise to question him too closely the way he was waving the pistol barrel about as he gestured. His red face looked whiter than when I'd seen him earlier this evening but his eyes were still angry.

"How did you get on to me, Mr Faraday?"

"I didn't," I said. "But something just came to me earlier tonight. You were the only one who saw the girl pass out the gate. After she left Larsen's it was like the earth had swallowed her up. She never left here, right?"

Simon nodded. The moisture was still glistening in his eyes. A board up near the fireplace creaked in the silence.

"What did you do with the car?" I said.

"Ran it over a cliff," he said. "There's a place about half a mile down. It fell into deep water. No-one was likely to find it there."

I drew deeply on the cigarette, sending long streamers of blue smoke up toward the library ceiling, thinking of a lot of things.

"Hadn't you better tell me about it?" I said.

Simon sat down on the edge of a big padded chair. He still kept the pistol in my general direction. I looked over toward the other end of the library. The Smith-Wesson was lying about a foot out from the edge of the book stack. A shadow crawled at the corner of my eye. I looked toward the big man and engaged his attention.

He blinked his eyes and focused on me like he was finding it difficult.

"What is there to tell?" he said.

"Just about everything," I said. "You told me Dale Holden was your wife."

He nodded. "She was no good. I knew that, really. All my friends told me so. She was in a jam at the time so she was glad to get married and leave San Francisco."

"That's where you met?"

The big man bit his lip.

262

"Sure. She owed Marcos money. She'd been dancing in a club he ran there. He was crazy about her too. So he followed us here."

Simon drew the sleeve of his windcheater across his big raw face.

"You see, Mr Faraday, she was a nympho. Any guy was fair game to her. It drove me crazy. But she seemed all right at first. And I believed her."

"You set Larsen up?" I said.

The big man nodded.

"He saw her dancing in a cheap club downtown. He didn't know we were married, of course. We didn't tell anybody. She told him some story and got me the job here as gateman. We both moved in earlier this year."

"What was the plan?" I said.

Simon looked moodily from me to the windows and then around the shadowy library. The house was silent. It seemed incredible that no-one had come in response to the storm of violence which had taken place here.

"We were going to take Larsen for

everything we could get. Dale told me about the payroll. We thought there might be as much as 200,000 in high notes."

"But Marcos followed and threatened to spoil the plan," I said.

The big man swallowed.

"It wasn't quite like that, Mr Faraday. But he was crazy about Dale. He'd been up here a few times and was becoming a nuisance. It threatened to blow our whole operation."

"Did he know you two were married?" I said.

Simon shook his head.

"Hardly anyone knew that, Mr Faraday. We kept it pretty close."

"But you were jealous?" I said.

Simon licked his lips again.

"You didn't know Dale, Mr Faraday. You had to possess her completely or leave her alone. She had a way of driving a man mad."

"I can imagine," I said, remembering the blurred photograph of the showgirl, and the portrait Lauritzen had showed me. I looked over toward the Smith-Wesson; the shadow had shifted position by now.

"Marcos was endangering your whole operation," I said. "You couldn't have that. So you went to his apartment and shot him. You left my business card for Joey and his friend to find."

Simon shrugged.

"It was dog eat dog, Mr Faraday. I knew Joey was after the money too. He came sniffing around the lodge once or twice. But he didn't dare try anything on the estate or I'd have told Larsen my suspicions."

"It was a nice little set-up," I said. "You almost got me killed."

Surprisingly, Simon suddenly grinned; he looked almost likeable at that moment.

"That was the idea, Mr Faraday. I heard from Dexter that Marcos had been trying to hire you to poke around."

I stood silent for a moment, digesting the information.

"So what went wrong?"

"Dale," Simon said simply. "She

couldn't keep her paws off anything that wore trousers. I knew there was something between her and the secretary."

"Lauritzen?"

"They were pretty close. And I knew Dale too well to trust her, particularly where two hundred thousand grand was concerned. We planned it pretty carefully. The money was already packed in cases, in high denomination notes. She was supposed to get it ready in Larsen's study for the pay-off. Instead, she brought it in the boot of her car down to me at the lodge."

I looked at him for a long moment. The wind was gusting now. A faint shadow crawled across behind the book stack.

"So you played it by ear?"

Simon got up. He looked gigantic under the light of the shaded lamp.

"I'd been drinking. Not too much but just enough to give me courage and to make me think clearly. The thing was going too easily. And jealousy is a terrible master. I'd been a private dick, like you. I was in the habit of making quick decisions in risky situations. We unloaded the cases in the living room of the lodge. I figured she was going to use me and then ditch me and go off with Lauritzen and the money."

"You told her that, of course?"

The big man looked at me with sombre eyes.

"It was a mistake. We got into a big argument. And me with a fortune in my hands and Larsen due back at the estate within the hour. She admitted the affair with Lauritzen. I just lost my head. I got her round the throat. I was mad with rage. When I came around she was dead."

I stood with my eyes fixed up near a corner of the ceiling; there was such misery in his voice there didn't seem anything to say. Simon went on in tones so low I had to strain to catch what he was saying.

"I'd already dug a hole in a small wood near the lodge to stash the money. I knew there would be a lot of heat on. But I figured Larsen would never suspect his gateman. And I had a story to account for Dale's disappearance. Jack Larsen never knew of any connection between the girl and me."

"So you buried her with the money?" I said.

The big man's eyes were haunted.

"It was the only way. It took me just a quarter of an hour longer to enlarge the hole. When I'd put things to rights I drove her car out and over the bluff. I'd been back in the lodge quite a while when Larsen came in."

"So you told him your story about Dale driving out," I said. "You were lucky. Why didn't you just put the girl in the car?"

Simon shook his head.

"Supposing the heap had been found in the sea. Sure, the girl would have been there. But no money. Where would that have left me?"

I finished off my cigarette and stubbed it out under my heel. There was enough mess on the floor. A little more wouldn't make any difference.

"You've got a point," I said. "All the while the car wasn't found both the girl and the money were together."

I looked him full in the face. He was the first to drop his eyes.

"And then I came around and not only Larsen but me and Joey and Gecko were all looking for the same thing. And you were sitting down at the gate with a fortune in your grasp and your wife out there dead and you unable to make a move. You poor bastard."

Some of the anger was back in Simon's eyes now.

"No need to feel sorry for me, Mr Faraday. I'm a rich man."

"If you get away with it," I said.

The man in the blue windcheater smiled slowly.

"I'll get away with it, Mr Faraday."

I had a sudden thought then.

"You took a picture of your wife and Marcos together out of Marcos's apartment?"

"Sure I did. What's it to you?"

"Just tying up the ends," I said. "Why did you put me on to Alys?"

"To take the heat off," he said.

A white hand was moving out the shadow now, toward the Smith-Wesson. Simon had his back to that part of the room. He was too absorbed to notice anything anyway. I went on talking, more to hold his attention than anything else. Simon was standing as though deep in thought. He sighed heavily.

"I'm real sorry about this, Mr Faraday."

"About what?" I said.

He gestured with the pistol.

"About everything."

He looked at me sadly, the muzzle of the gun coming up.

"I got to do it, Mr Faraday."

"Don't be a fool," I said.

I looked round the room.

"There's been enough already. What do you think it will solve?"

Simon shook his head.

"It will solve most of my problems. With the money I can get to South America. We'll just take a little walk in the grounds. I shall need you to do the digging."

"All right," I said.

I moved over toward the French windows. The Smith-Wesson was coming up off the floor now. Simon turned at the slight sound, surprise on his face. He brought the gun up, his face an angry knot of concentration. The Smith-Wesson roared, the bullet whining angrily round the walls. Chips of plaster flew about and the smoke seemed to fill the room.

I went across the floor in a long dive. I caught Simon round the knees before he got the pistol up. We both went down with a crash that shook the building. Then I had his gun-hand, hammering it against the leg of a table. The pistol skidded across the parquet as the frightened face of Greg Lauritzen showed.

"You took your time," I told him.

20

THE secretary looked sick. He glanced around the room like he couldn't believe what his eyes were telling him. He passed his tongue over dry lips and absently handed me the Smith-Wesson muzzle first. I removed it quickly before something came out the barrel. He looked at Simon on the floor nursing his wrist.

"O my God, O my God," he said over and over in a monotonous voice.

"You did all right," I told him. "Remind me to thank you when this is all over. In the meantime you better have your story ready for the law."

"The law?"

Lauritzen's eyes focused on my face with difficulty.

"The law," I repeated. "The boys in blue. You must have heard of them.

They'll be swarming all over here in a little while."

Lauritzen shook his head.

"I've done nothing wrong, Mr Faraday."

"Glad to hear it," I told him. "Then you've got nothing to worry about."

The big man in the blue windcheater was getting up now. I held the Smith-Wesson on him, gestured him down into a chair. I walked over and collected his cannon and put it in my pocket. Lauritzen had gotten control of himself by now.

"I heard everything," he said. "I was behind the bookcase. I swear I didn't know anything about Dale being married to him. Or the money."

"Don't worry," I said again. "She double-crossed everybody. She would only have crossed you even if you had been in it. This poor bastard was the one who had the misfortune to marry her."

I went and stood looking down at him.

"We'd better go get the money. This time you'll start the digging."

Simon didn't say anything. He was nursing his wrist and all the anger had gone out of his eyes. Now they only looked sick.

"How did you come to be here?" I asked Lauritzen. "You couldn't have heard the racket, according to Simon."

Lauritzen shook his head.

"I tried to phone the gate earlier tonight. There was no reply. That was unusual in itself. So I thought I'd find out from Mr Larsen what was going on."

"Good thing you did," I said. "You saved my life."

I took my eyes off Simon, looked at the secretary steadily.

"Maybe I had you figured all wrong." I sighed.

"It was all of a piece with the case."

Lauritzen hesitantly put out his hand. I shook it. My amused expression seemed to shock him.

"My sense of humour," I told him. "The only person in the case who was levelling I'd picked as a phoney."

Lauritzen smiled too.

"What about all this?" he said.

"Don't worry," I told him. "I'll go to bat for you when the time comes."

Lauritzen smiled too.

"There are one or two little things in my past I wouldn't like the police probing into. Perhaps my somewhat nervous attitude aroused your suspicion."

"Could be," I said. "In the meantime you'd better ring the law while I take a look down at the lodge."

He nodded and went over to the phone, avoiding looking at the mess on the floor. I looked around the library again, thinking of Larsen and Joey and the panther and Simon and now Lauritzen.

"We should have sold tickets," I said.

"Eh?"

Lauritzen looked puzzled.

"Nothing," I told him. "We'll be down at the lodge. I'll leave the gates open for the police."

I put the Smith-Wesson up, waited for Simon to precede me through the window.

"If that panther shows up again you'll be the first one to get it," I said.

A diesel generator was throbbing somewhere in the background. The light, almost white in its brilliance, shone down on the clearing among the dark trees. Simon sat on a tree-stump with his head in his hands. Two big police officers were enlarging the hole with trenching tools. A six feet-three sergeant with a halo of frosty hair chewed on an unlit cigar and watched them.

A plain-clothes Lieutenant I knew called McGiver stood a little way off with a thin, bald-headed police surgeon and conversed in low tones. Lauritzen and I stood smoking by the side of one of the police cars whose headlights added detail to the scene.

I noticed he was trembling. I went back up to the house. That was swarming with police too. Flashbulbs were popping and throwing white light on to the walls of the library. I found what I wanted, took four glasses and went back down to the lodge. There was a swarm of reporters at the gates. Three big patrolmen were keeping stony faces in spite of the barrage of questions.

Lauritzen turned to me gratefully as I splashed the whisky in the glass. He drained it in two gulps and held out the glass for another.

"God, I needed this," he said.

I poured myself a shot, put it down on the bonnet of the car. I took the bottle over to McGiver and the surgeon. McGiver's face broke out in a brief smile.

"Great, Mr Faraday."

He toasted me over the rim of his glass.

"Lauritzen's worried," I said, looking over toward the hole. The diggers were lifting out two big suitcases now. Simon was sitting upright, his face drained of all colour in the light of the lamps.

"He needn't be," McGiver said. "So far as I can see, he's in the clear."

I nodded. McGiver looked at me sharply.

"He's not to leave town."

"Sure," I said.

"That goes for you too," McGiver said.

I grinned. I went over to where Simon sat. He waved the bottle away. Something wrapped in burlap was coming into view now. The onlookers suddenly started moving in toward the hole. It had now assumed the aspect of a grave. I went back to join Lauritzen. I'd rather remember the girl in the photographs. That reminded me of something else.

"You're in the clear," I told Lauritzen. "But you'd better give the police your address before you leave."

He nodded.

"I'm grateful, Mr Faraday. I'll ride back in with you if you don't mind. I couldn't face driving in my state of mind."

I went over to the Buick. I'd parked it down near the end of the drive when the law arrived. I'd clean forgotten until now. I unlocked the dash cubby and took out the envelope. I carried it back up to

Lauritzen. He stood frowning, his hands tightly clenched round the glass, looking toward the backs of the people clustered around the hole.

He opened up the envelope and looked at the contents uncomprehendingly. Then he took the photographs of Dale Holden and tore them across. I didn't say anything but picked up my drink and finished it off. I felt life coming back into me. I stood and watched him scatter the pieces of the photographs to the winds. It was almost dawn and there was a heavy dew.

"You coming?" I said. "There's nothing to keep us here now."

"Sure," he said. "I'll pick up my car and my personal stuff when the heat dies down."

He walked over to McGiver. I went and sat in the car and waited for him. When he re-joined me I drove to another entrance a couple of miles down, with Lauritzen directing me. He had his own bunch of keys and unlocked the metal-grilled gate. The sun was coming up as we started making time in to L.A. I felt and no doubt looked a wreck. I dropped Lauritzen off at a small hotel and watched him inside.

Then I drove across town and dropped the Buick in the usual garage. I walked back a couple of blocks and found a coffee shop. I got outside some ham and eggs, waffles and syrup and three big cups of coffee. I felt better then. I looked at my watch. It was already half-past nine.

I could hear Stella's typewriter clacking as I came down the corridor. She looked at my face without a word and went quickly over to the alcove.

"You look rough, Mike."

"I feel rough," I said.

I told her what had happened. She stood, her arms folded, the light from the blinds making a blonde halo of her hair. Her eyes were very blue.

"I'll make some coffee," she said.

"Fine," I said. Another cup never hurt.

I went and sat down in my chair behind the desk. It was only then I realized how tired I was.

"You ought to go home to bed, Mike," Stella said.

She went back behind the frosted glass screen.

"I will, just as soon as I've finished the report," I said.

I dictated it to her over the coffee, omitting nothing. Stella didn't say anything for a while after I'd finished, but there was a strange look around her eyes I'd seen once or twice before. She got up and came over to me. Her lips brushed my forehead. I held her close to me for a long minute. Then she pulled away and went back to her own desk.

"They were a nice crowd of people," she said.

"As nice as they come," I said. "And by and large they got what they deserved."

I set fire to a cigarette and looked across to the window and down to the boulevard where the stalled traffic was making nice snarl-ups already.

"Leastways, we came out a thousand dollars to the good," I said. I feathered blue smoke at the ceiling and sat watching the traffic, thinking about nothing in particular now.

"She must have been quite a girl," Stella said softly.

I nodded.

"I can't think of the word for the moment."

I had another idea then. I got Stella to dial the hotel where I'd dropped Lauritzen. He came on the line straight away, so he hadn't gotten to bed.

"Something I just thought of," I told him. "You might drop over to see Alys Vermilyea. She seemed quite a nice woman. It would come better from you."

There was a long silence on the wire. Then his voice came over strong and clear.

"You may have something there, Mr Faraday. It had crossed my mind. You think we might console one another?"

I grinned.

"A woman like that's too good to waste. And in my book you'd both be getting better value than what you lost."

"Nice of you to say so," Lauritzen said. "I'll tell you how I make out."

He put the phone down. Stella sat drinking her coffee, the sunlight bright on the gold bell of her hair, that enigmatic expression on her face I'd gotten to know so well. She looked at my battered face thoughtfully.

"You were lucky, Mike."

I smiled.

"It's the Year of the Dragon," I said.

THE END

Other titles in the
Linford Mystery Library:

A GENTEEL LITTLE MURDER
Philip Daniels

Gilbert had a long-cherished plan to murder his wife. When the polished Edward entered the scene Gilbert's attitude was suddenly changed.

DEATH AT THE WEDDING
Madelaine Duke

Dr. Norah North's search for a killer takes her from a wedding to a private hospital.

MURDER FIRST CLASS
Ron Ellis

Will Detective Chief Inspector Glass find the Post Office robbers before the Executioner gets to them?

A FOOT IN THE GRAVE
Bruce Marshall

About to be imprisoned and tortured in Buenos Aires, John Smith escapes, only to become involved in an aeroplane hijacking.

DEAD TROUBLE
Martin Carroll

Trespassing brought Jennifer Denning more than she bargained for. She was totally unprepared for the violence which was to lie in her path.

HOURS TO KILL
Ursula Curtiss

Margaret went to New Mexico to look after her sick sister's rented house and felt a sharp edge of fear when the absent landlady arrived.

THE DEATH OF ABBE DIDIER
Richard Grayson

Inspector Gautier of the Sûreté investigates three crimes which are strangely connected.

NIGHTMARE TIME
Hugh Pentecost

Have the missing major and his wife met with foul play somewhere in the Beaumont Hotel, or is their disappearance a carefully planned step in an act of treason?

BLOOD WILL OUT
Margaret Carr

Why was the manor house so oddly familiar to Elinor Howard? Who would have guessed that a Sunday School outing could lead to murder?

THE DRACULA MURDERS
Philip Daniels

The Horror Ball was interrupted by a spectral figure who warned the merrymakers they were tampering with the unknown.

THE LADIES
OF LAMBTON GREEN
Liza Shepherd

Why did murdered Robin Colquhoun's picture pose such a threat to the ladies of Lambton Green?

CARNABY
AND THE GAOLBREAKERS
Peter N. Walker

Detective Sergeant James Aloysius Carnaby-King is sent to prison as bait. When he joins in an escape he is thrown headfirst into a vicious murder hunt.

MUD IN HIS EYE
Gerald Hammond

The harbourmaster's body is found mangled beneath Major Smyle's yacht. What is the sinister significance of the illicit oysters?

THE SCAVENGERS
Bill Knox

Among the masses of struggling fish in the *Tecta*'s nets was a larger, darker, ominously motionless form . . . the body of a skin diver.

DEATH IN ARCADY
Stella Phillips

Detective Inspector Matthew Furnival works unofficially with the local police when a brutal murder takes place in a caravan camp.

STORM CENTRE
Douglas Clark

Detective Chief Superintendent Masters, temporarily lecturing in a police staff college, finds there's more to the job than a few weeks relaxation in a rural setting.

THE MANUSCRIPT MURDERS
Roy Harley Lewis

Antiquarian bookseller Matthew Coll, acquires a rare 16th century manuscript. But when the Dutch professor who had discovered the journal is murdered, Coll begins to doubt its authenticity.

SHARENDEL
Margaret Carr

Ruth didn't want all that money. And she didn't want Aunt Cass to die. But at Sharendel things looked different. She began to wonder if she had a split personality.

MURDER TO BURN
Laurie Mantell

Sergeants Steven Arrow and Lance Brendon, of the New Zealand police force, come upon a woman's body in the water. When the dead woman is identified they begin to realise that they are investigating a complex fraud.

YOU CAN HELP ME
Maisie Birmingham

Whilst running the Citizens' Advice Bureau, Kate Weatherley is attacked with no apparent motive. Then the body of one of her clients is found in her room.

DAGGERS DRAWN
Margaret Carr

Stacey Manston was the kind of girl who could take most things in her stride, but three murders were something different . . .

THE MONTMARTRE MURDERS
Richard Grayson

Inspector Gautier of Sûreté investigates the disappearance of artist Théo, the heir to a fortune.

GRIZZLY TRAIL
Gwen Moffat

Miss Pink, alone in the Rockies, helps in a search for missing hikers, solves two cruel murders and has the most terrifying experience of her life when she meets a grizzly bear!

BLINDMAN'S BLUFF
Margaret Carr

Kate Deverill had considered suicide. It was one way out — and preferable to being murdered.

BEGOTTEN MURDER
Martin Carroll

When Susan Phillips joined her aunt on a voyage of 12,000 miles from her home in Melbourne, she little knew their arrival would germinate the seeds of murder planted long ago.

WHO'S THE TARGET?
Margaret Carr

Three people whom Abby could identify as her parents' murderers wanted her dead, but she decided that maybe Jason could have been the target.

THE LOOSE SCREW
Gerald Hammond

After a motor smash, Beau Pepys and his cousin Jacqueline, her fiancé and dotty mother, suspect that someone had prearranged the death of their friend. But who, and why?

CASE WITH THREE HUSBANDS
Margaret Erskine

Was it a ghost of one of Rose Bonner's late husbands that gave her old Aunt Agatha such a terrible shock and then murdered her in her bed?

THE END OF THE RUNNING
Alan Evans

Lang continued to push the men and children on and on. Behind them were the men who were hunting them down, waiting for the first signs of exhaustion before they pounced.

CARNABY AND THE HIJACKERS
Peter N. Walker

When Commander Pigeon assigns Detective Sergeant Carnaby-King to prevent a raid on a bullion-carrying passenger train, he knows that there are traitors in high positions.

TREAD WARILY AT MIDNIGHT
Margaret Carr

If Joanna Morse hadn't been so hasty she wouldn't have been involved in the accident.

TOO BEAUTIFUL TO DIE
Martin Carroll

There was a grave in the churchyard to prove Elizabeth Weston was dead. Alive, she presented a problem. Dead, she could be forgotten. Then, in the eighth year of her death she came back. She was beautiful, but she had to die.

IN COLD PURSUIT
Ursula Curtiss

In Mexico, Mary and her cousin Jenny each encounter strange men, but neither of them realises that one of these men is obsessed with revenge and murder. But which one?

LITTLE DROPS OF BLOOD
Bill Knox

It might have been just another unfortunate road accident but a few little drops of blood pointed to murder.

GOSSIP TO THE GRAVE
Jonathan Burke

Jenny Clark invented Simon Sherborne because her daily gossip column was getting dull. Then Simon appeared at a party — in the flesh! And Jenny finds herself involved in murder.

HARRIET FAREWELL
Margaret Erskine

Wealthy Theodore Buckler had planned a magnificent Guy Fawkes Day celebration. He hadn't planned on murder.

SANCTUARY ISLE
Bill Knox

Chief Detective Inspector Colin Thane and Detective Inspector Phil Moss are sent to a bird sanctuary off the coast of Argyll to investigate the murder of the warden.

THE SNOW ON THE BEN
Ian Stuart

Although on holiday in the Highlands, Chief Inspector Hamish MacLeod begins an investigation when a pistol shot shatters the quiet of his solitary morning walk.

HARD CONTRACT
Basil Copper

Private detective Mike Farraday is hired to obtain settlement of a debt from Minsky. But Minsky is killed before Mike can get to him. A spate of murders follows.